DISCOVERED DECEPTION

DISCOVERED DECEPTION

THE DISCOVERED TRUTH SERIES ROMANTIC SUSPENSE
BOOK EIGHT

JULIE BAWDEN DAVIS

Roses
ARE
RED
PUBLISHING

Cover by Judy Bullard (customebookcovers.com)

Book design by Jeremy Davis

Palm logo design by Kayla Curry

Roses are Red logo design by Kyle Kane

ISBN-13: 978-1-955265-25-6

ISBN: 1-955265-25-9

Distributed by Roses Are Red Publishing

rosesareredpublishing.com

❀ Created with Vellum

ACKNOWLEDGMENTS

As they say, it takes a village. Here's my village. I'm supremely grateful to each of these fabulous people!

ARC Reviewers
Julie Schlueter
Tara Bradley
Heather Wamboldt
Susa Fraccaroli
Kery Bailey
Trish Darrenkamp
Marilyn Smith
Lisa Starkey
Amber Mancebo

Pros
Sharon Whatley, editing
Judy Bullard, cover design
Kayla Curry, logo design
Kyle Kane, logo design
Sabrina Wildermuth, design consultation
Jeremy Davis, book design

To my mother, Lynn, whose love of diamonds outshines them all.

PROLOGUE

LAKE BLUE RIDGE, GEORGIA

August 19, 1999

Susa ran to the tree in the field, panting, her side aching. She didn't want to be late. Hermann had insisted they meet when the moon hit a certain position in the sky. If they were off by even a minute, he said their plan wouldn't work. When she got to the clearing and saw the tree in the moonlight, she noted two figures already there. Rogue and her cousin. Her heart quickened when she thought about seeing Rogue under the stars.

"We were beginning to think you weren't going to make it, hon," said Hermann when Susa came running up.

She stopped and clutched her side, gasping her response. "I'm sorry, but my mother wouldn't go to bed. I thought she'd be up all night."

"Weren't you going to climb out of your window?" said Rogue, his dark eyes meeting hers. Her heart rate sped up even more. Resisting the urge to check her hair, which she'd spent an hour straightening in an attempt to tame it into submission against the damp Georgia air, she replied with a lie. "My mother was outside on the front porch." The truth was, she was scared to scale down the side of the lake house like Rogue had suggested.

He nodded in understanding, and she let out a sigh of relief.

"Well, I'm glad we're all here," said Hermann, reaching his hands toward the sky. "Are you both ready?"

Susa and Rogue solemnly nodded. Susa pulled a napkin out of her pocket, unwrapping it carefully to expose a white stone. Rogue also reached into his pocket, pulling out another stone. His was jet-black. She blinked when his stone glinted in the moonlight.

After surveying their offerings, Hermann opened a purple velvet cloth and took out a diamond ring, handing the cloth and ring to Susa. He picked up a shovel and went to the side of the giant oak and began digging. When he'd created a hole a foot deep, he asked them to bring the items.

"First, Susa, hold the ring up to the moon. Even if it's cubic zirconia, it'll catch the light."

Susa did as Hermann instructed, watching as the moonlight danced off the ring and the gem sparkled. She wrapped the ring back up in the velvety cloth and handed it and the stone to Hermann, who put them in a small box. Then he pointed to Rogue, who responded by holding up his stone and turning it. He handed the stone to Hermann, who put it in the box, which he closed and set into the earth. Then Rogue took the shovel and covered the box with soil.

"Susa, it's your turn to pat down the earth," said Hermann in a stage whisper. She got down on her hands and knees and patted down the soil until it looked like nothing had disturbed the area. Standing, she wiped the dirt from her hands.

"Come," said Hermann, reaching for each of their hands. "It's time."

As they left the shadow of the tree, Susa took Hermann's hand and Rogue's. When Rogue's hand enveloped hers, she felt a delicious shiver run up and down her spine. She stole a glance at him, but his eyes remained on Hermann, who had put his face up to the moonlit sky.

"We shall meet here at this exact spot in the year 2019," said Hermann in a monotone. "By then, magical things will have come to pass in our lives. We will see one another, and we won't recognize one another, and yet we will recognize one another."

Hermann removed his hands from theirs, and Susa reluctantly let go of Rogue's warm grasp. They left the tree in silence, each making their way home alone. She was used to Hermann's games, and had no idea the meaning of what they had just done. All she knew was that she wanted to hold Rogue's hand again. But that was the last time Susa saw Rogue that summer.

IRVINE, CALIFORNIA

DECEMBER 19, 2019

Susa York leaned over the microscope again, hoping to see a different outcome. The plant receptors still weren't responding. What had she done wrong? She sat back on the laboratory stool. She'd cut the specimens carefully. There couldn't have been any contamination.

Her phone buzzed, and she grabbed it from her laboratory table, reading the text message from her sister. *Where are you? Don and I are at the restaurant. Did you forget again?*

"Oh, darn," Susa said aloud to the empty laboratory. She turned off the microscope and put away the slide, then rushed to the door. Pulling off her lab coat, she hung it on a hook next to the others. Grabbing the clipboard from the wall, she scribbled her name, then left to cross the campus. As she walked, she smoothed down her hair, glad to feel that it wasn't frizzing much in the dry Southern California air. She hopped in her Mini Cooper and pulled out of the University of California, Irvine parking lot onto Culver. Before long, she spotted the Italian restaurant where they were meeting and parked. Jumping out of the car, she glanced down with dismay to see a stain from lunch on her pants. She covered the dark spot with her purse, then walked into the restaurant. Christmas music piped in overhead, and the hostess greeted her with a smile.

"I'm looking for a couple who came in a while ago. The name is Sanders."

"Oh, yes, the couple and another man." The woman turned, beckoning Susa to follow. "They said you might be arriving late."

Ugh, Susa thought. Cathy had done it again. Another blind date. Forcing a wooden smile on her face, she followed the hostess to a table where she saw her sister and brother-in-law and a balding guy with glasses.

"Susa, so glad you could make it. This is Roger," Cathy said as she and the man stood. Roger reached to take Susa's hand with his cool one.

"Very nice to meet you," said Susa, juggling her purse as she shook his hand, sure that she had exposed her soy sauce stain. Her sister motioned for her to slide into the booth next to Roger, while she took a seat beside her husband, Don.

"Well, this is nice and cozy," said Cathy. "We ordered some appetizers."

Susa nodded, wishing there was a time machine that could speed this dinner up, so she could get back to her experiment.

"Cathy says you're a scientist," said Roger. "What do you study?"

"Plant dynamics, focusing on their ability to help access certain human genomes, hopefully leading to answers as to why people develop various illnesses, and perhaps even to see if those illnesses can be accessed in the body before they take hold, using plant sequencing."

"Oh, um, that sounds very interesting," said Roger as the waitress put a big platter of calamari on the table. He averted his eyes from Susa and began filling his plate with squid tendrils.

"What my sister, the scientist, is trying to say is that plants and humans have the same DNA. She's studying plants to learn more about people."

Roger's face brightened. "Oh, I see."

Susa studied his features, noting that he appeared to be suffering from male pattern baldness. As she recalled, that was a recessive gene.

"Earth to Susa. Did you want some wine?" Cathy chirped.

Susa looked up to see the waitress hovering over her with a notepad in hand. "A chardonnay would be nice." Her mind continued humming. She wondered if all the men in Roger's family were bald.

"Roger is a salesman," said Cathy.

"Oh," said Susa, after she swallowed a mouthful of calamari. "What do you sell?"

Roger seemed a bit uncomfortable before replying, "Shoes. I work at a shoe store in the mall."

"How nice," said Susa, unsure what to say to that. An awkward silence ensued. She breathed a sigh of relief when the waitress returned with her wine. Taking it, Susa swallowed several generous mouthfuls and put the glass on the table.

An hour later, Susa stood by her car with Cathy as Don waited in their car. "I know you mean well, Cathy, but these blind dates have got to stop."

Her sister sighed and looked up at the sky. "I'm just trying to help. Do you want to be alone for the rest of your life?"

"I'm only thirty-seven. You're talking as if I'm eighty." She nodded her head in the direction of Roger's receding taillights. "I don't want to die of boredom."

"Okay, maybe a shoe salesman wasn't the best idea. It's hard to find scientists."

"It's not your job. You need to get back home. I'm sure Devan is still up driving his sitter crazy," said Susa of her nephew. She gave Cathy a quick hug.

"So, you're not mad at me?"

Susa laughed. "The last time I remember being mad at you was when you put sugar in my underwear drawer."

"I was only seven years old," said Cathy, laughing at the memory. She held up one hand as she backed up to leave. "I swear, no more shoe salesmen. I'll see you for Christmas dinner. You did remember that it's this coming Saturday, I hope?"

"Of course," said Susa as she got in her car. Was Christmas that soon? Then she waved and drove onto the street. Within ten minutes, she pulled into the driveway of her low-slung California ranch-style home and shut off the engine.

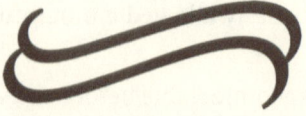

Kent Aronson turned off the restaurant grill and sighed. It had been a hard, long night. The dinner hours the week before Christmas always resulted in a double workload with people out shopping and wanting something good to eat. Orders had come in faster than he could cook them, and with his sous chef out, he hadn't sat down once all night. His back and feet ached as a result. It was ironic to Kent that this work was so hard on him physically. He'd left racing to save his body. Especially after the last fiery crash. Shaking off the memory and the painful facial reconstructive surgery that followed, he did a final check to ensure that all kitchen appliances were off, then hit the light switch. Pushing open the kitchen's swinging doors, he stepped out into the front of the restaurant. He liked this time of night when everyone had left, and he could finally think. The server and busboy had prepped the tables for the next day. The white napkins lay neatly folded next to each plate, the wine glasses standing at attention.

He went behind the bar, which looked out over the dining room, all decked out for the holidays. Pouring himself a shot of whiskey neat, he swallowed it with one gulp. Sales had been good, so he couldn't complain. Good reviews online about the restaurant, as well. Every December as the year wound down, though, he couldn't help but take stock of his personal life. Another Christmas alone with no family of his own, except for his sister. He walked over and turned the lights off on the Christmas tree that filled a corner of the room, then locked up and headed for home.

2

Susa set her purse on the side table in the entryway. She knew what came next. A long night with her mind whirring about why that sequence hadn't worked. She eyed the clock on the wall. Only nine-thirty. She had an early meeting tomorrow with her boss, but she could easily run back to the lab right now, for just another hour. She hit the light switch and shut the door.

After forty-five fruitless minutes, Susa rubbed the back of her neck with her hand and stared through the microscope again, letting her eyes lose their focus. Sometimes when she did that, she'd spot an anomaly. As her heart sped up at the possibilities she saw, her phone buzzed. Who on earth could be contacting her at this late hour? She picked up her cell from the laboratory table. Her cousin, Hermann.

"Hermann? What's going on?"

"So glad you answered. I've got a bit of a problem."

Susa scooted to the edge of the stool she'd been sitting on. "You okay? You sound kind of strange."

"I'm fine. It's just a little snafu. Something got dumped in my lap yesterday, and now I'm not sure what to do with it."

"So, you call me? What about your partner in crime, Irena?"

"She's in Colorado right now."

Susa sat back on the stool and waited to hear the rest.

"I wouldn't have called you if I had any other choice. You know that."

"Actually Hermann, I don't know that. I could have lost my scholarship the last time I helped you."

"This is different. I just need you to hold some items for me, for a little while. Nothing treacherous. They'll fit in the palm of your hand. You'd be a lifesaver."

Susa contemplated his request.

"Look, if you don't want to, I understand. It's just that if Brad were to catch me with the little package—".

"Fine." Susa cut him off. "I can meet you tomorrow for lunch."

"Actually, I'm outside of UCI right now. I'm going to leave the bag behind the trashcan to the left of the front door. Come out in a minute and pretend to drop something, then get it. I don't think we should be seen together."

Alarm bells sounded in Susa's head. "Okay," she said, thinking how she didn't want to jeopardize his relationship with Brad. Hermann had settled down so much after getting together with him.

"You're a lifesaver," Hermann said, sounding greatly relieved. "I swear I'll pay you back."

"You've said lifesaver twice. It's making me nervous."

"Just an expression, hon. I'll be in touch."

Susa grabbed her purse and headed for the elevator, taking it to the first floor. When she walked out into the quiet night, she glanced around. No one in sight. She reached into her bag and pulled out a pen and notepad, then pretended to drop them on the ground. Kneeling, she rummaged around, spying a black bag behind the trashcan. She grabbed the bag and slid it into her purse, then headed home. Her cousin could be dramatic, with an appetite for getting in trouble. Since they were kids, he loved to pretend like he was a secret operative—and he loved making Susa play along even more.

"Isn't that your mom's wedding ring, Hermann?"

"Yes, I took it out of the cleaning solution she likes to soak it in."

"You need to put that back," said Susa, thirteen-years-old at the time. It was spring break, and she was visiting Hermann's house in Arizona.

"Don't be such a worry wart. I take it out all the time. Want to see something really cool?"

"Sure, fine, but make it quick."

"We need to go outside," said Hermann, who went running for the backyard. Susa followed him into the bright, hot sunlight and watched as he raised the diamond into the air. She gasped when sunlight refracted from the ring, creating a sprinkling of small colored orbs on the nearby sidewalk.

"It's magic," said Hermann.

"I don't think it's magic," said Susa. "It must have something to do with the way the diamond is cut."

"Yes, but it's still magical." Hermann spun around, then stopped. "Maybe I'll own a jewelry store one day."

"I thought you wanted to be an actor?"

"I'll do that, too."

"Okay, can you please put your mom's ring back now?"

"Fine. If it'll make you feel better, cuz." Hermann headed for the house, calling over his shoulder, "Let's go make hot fudge sundaes."

"Your mom said not to touch the ice cream. It's for dessert tonight." Susa ran into the house after her cousin.

When Susa got home and set down her things, she couldn't help thinking about Hermann's phone call. She knew her cousin well, and there was something about his voice tonight that made her feel unsettled. Most likely he was just concerned about messing up his relationship with Brad. Susa knew that Hermann had worked hard the last year to clean up his act. If she could help him stay on that path, what harm could it do to help him out?

Kent woke in the middle of the night, his back spasming, vestiges of the familiar dream still tugging at him. He saw in his mind's eye the steering wheel seeming to slide out of his grasp, and the car rolling. He reached around and massaged his back, glancing out of his floor to ceiling window at the smattering of stars in the sky. The night was quiet, save for a coyote howling in the foothills. Moving out to Trabuco Canyon was the best choice he'd made in years. The laid-back hippy vibe and undeveloped land had instantly appealed to his country upbringing in the Ozarks. That was before his parents died and he and his sister, Gloria, ended up moving all over the south.

Grimacing from pain as he sat up, Kent opened his bedside table drawer, pulling out a bottle of ibuprofen. He started to uncap it but changed his mind and threw the pain reliever back in the drawer. Instead, he got out of bed and put on a robe, then slid open the door to his deck, stepping out into the chilly night. Pulling the cover off his hot tub, he tested the temperature with his hand, then turned up the thermostat and powered on the jets. While waiting for the water to warm, he gazed up at the starry sky and nearly full moon, wondering as he always did when he looked at the night sky. Where was she now? Married with kids? Traveling the world? He really wished he knew.

3

Susa woke up to a ringing sound in the early morning. She fumbled around the bedside table until she located her phone. Hermann again.

"Why are you calling at this hour?" She flopped back on the pillow.

"Did you look inside the bag?"

Susa sighed as the veil of sleep slid away. "No, I didn't yet." She recalled the time when they were kids and Hermann had put a bag of Mexican jumping beans under her bed. She'd woken in the middle of the night convinced a bomb was ticking and about to explode.

"I think you should stash it at the lab. Stick it with some of your unused beakers or something." Hermann sounded out of breath.

"I'll figure a place for the bag, but when are you going to pick it up?"

"Soon. I'll be in touch." Then her cousin hung up.

Just like Hermann to wake her up with a mysterious phone call. She closed her eyes and tried slowly counting backwards from one hundred. When she was still wide awake at twenty, she decided to get up and shower and go into the lab.

In the bathroom, Susa turned on the track lighting over the mirror and checked her face. When she was young, she hated the freckles sprinkled across her nose. In college, though, she learned in genetics class that freckles were a dominant trait, and that made her respect them. Putting her long hair into a bun, she turned on the shower. As she bathed, Susa wondered about Hermann's phone call. He wasn't much of an early bird. Just what was in the bag?

When she finished showering, she got out and toweled off, then wrapped the towel around herself. She went to get her purse and brought it into the kitchen. Searching inside until she felt the bag, she pulled it out and set it on the counter, eyeing it as she filled and started the coffee machine. Hermann had in the past walked on what some might call the "wrong side of the law." Susa had never been involved in any of his escapades, but he would sometimes tell her about them. That was generally after the fact, though. She picked up the bag with one hand and shook it. Rocks?

Once she poured herself a cup of coffee and added a teaspoon of sugar, she took the bag to the kitchen table and sat down, loosening the drawstring top. Peering inside, she gasped. Diamonds. Laying the bag on its side, she shook at least forty to fifty gems onto the table, watching them glint in the kitchen light. She wasn't an expert, but these sure appeared real. Many were tinged purple. How much was all this worth? The last thing she needed was to have this bag discovered at the lab. Getting caught with potentially stolen gems could result in losing her grant funding, and even her job. Susa dialed Hermann's number. Her cousin's voicemail answered. She hung up and started a text, then stopped. Something told her not to leave a digital trail. Carefully, she put all the gems back into the bag and looked around her house for a hiding place. She decided on the bottom shelf of her bookcase, behind her molecular biology textbook.

"Go ahead and kiss him, already. You know you want to." She and Hermann were sitting on the porch swing of their Aunt Marion's lake house in Georgia. Susa grimaced at her long legs stretched out in front of her. They reminded her of chicken legs.

"Don't you dare tell him I like him. I'm sure he has a girlfriend, who is much prettier than me."

"Are you kidding? You're gorgeous. Do you know how many guys like redheads?"

Susa was silent.

"Fine, I won't be a buttinsky. I promise."

Susa swiveled to face her cousin, willing him to look her in the eyes. "Swear it."

Hermann raised his eyebrows. "You really do like this guy. I'm surprised. You usually have your head stuck in a book." Her cousin grinned. "He's a bad boy. You know that, right? Why do you think they call him Rogue?"

"I hadn't thought about it."

"Rumor is he stole his sister's car and crashed it into a tree. And the two of them have been raising themselves. Their parents died or left or something."

"I'm sure he had a reason for taking his sister's car."

Her cousin shook his head and tsk-tsked. "You're smitten."

Susa sat up straight and put her face inches from Hermann's. "Swear to me that you will never tell him I like him. Or I'll tell your mom that..." She trailed off and looked away.

"That I like boys?" Hermann spoke in a low voice as he glanced at the screen door.

"I didn't mean that," she mumbled, immediately feeling ashamed. She turned to look at him. "You know I'd never do that."

Hermann's hazel eyes softened. "I know. I solemnly swear that I, Hermann St. James, will never, ever, under any circumstances, let Rogue know that Susa is madly in love with him."

4

It was quiet in the lab, except for the holiday music piping in. Susa pulled a box containing spliced rose hips toward her. Using tweezers, she removed the plant matter, putting it on a slide and under the microscope. There were newer machines she could be using, but Susa liked to go old school sometimes. She especially loved classic microscopes. It might be her imagination, but there was something about using the naked eye and the power of perception that the newer machines just couldn't accomplish.

With the gene sequencing work she'd been doing for the past three years, she sometimes felt like she wasn't moving fast enough. But then she reminded herself what her mentor always said. "Great discoveries come from hours of refined, exact, precise study." Susa had put plenty of hours into doing just that. According to her sister, way too many hours. But one day, when Susa's name was associated with a discovery, her sister might change her tune.

As she made notes on what she saw in the slide, Susa's coworkers began to file in for the day. Bernard, a tall fellow scientist with a pile of blond hair on his head, sidled up to her. "I can take a look if you want another set of eyes." He smelled like the spearmint gum he constantly chewed.

"Sure, go ahead. I'm looking for sequencing that might replicate that genome I found the other day." She scooted out of the way so he could peer through the lens.

"There seems to be a fiber running around the edge. I'm not sure if it's significant." He unfolded himself and looked down at Susa. She sometimes thought Bernard might have a crush on her, but she didn't return the feeling.

"Thanks. I'll check it out." She motioned to look, and he got the hint. Before he went to his own workstation, he added, "You going to the lab holiday dinner tonight?"

Susa's face must have betrayed her, because he grinned. "You forgot. Good thing you have me to remind you of these things."

"I'll be there." She opened her laboratory table drawer and rifled around for the invitation. "Where exactly is the dinner?"

"A restaurant on McFadden. The Tipping Whale. Supposed to have good food. Six o'clock."

Susa nodded, her mind wandering back to her study. Something about that stray fiber reminded her of a DNA study that she'd read in a microbiology book. Maybe she could find it in the science library.

Kent opened the doors of the restaurant to the smell of coffee brewing and bread baking.

"That you?" Ernesto, his baker, sous chef and right-hand man, called from the kitchen.

"Last time I checked." Kent pushed through the swinging doors to find Ernesto leaning over a plate of steaming eggs and bacon at the butcher block. "There's coffee, if you want," he said between bites.

Kent poured himself a big mug and pulled open the subzero refrigerator to find the half-and-half. Splashing a dollop into his coffee, he held up the carton. "You want any?"

Ernesto shook his head. "Trying to cut back on the fats."

Kent eyed his plate and laughed. "I can see that. How's your mom?"

Ernesto glanced up from eating and swallowed. "Thanks for the time off. I know it was tough for you yesterday. She's doing better. The doctors have the pneumonia under control now."

"That's good." Kent changed the subject, figuring that Ernesto had said all he would. "So, what's on the agenda for today?"

"Start prepping for that private event tonight."

"That's right, the UCI lab holiday party. It's been awhile since we planned the menu. Remind me what we decided to make."

"Braised duck on a bed of arugula. The other main dish is pork medallions with a balsamic glaze." Ernesto pushed a piece of cardboard toward Kent, where he'd scribbled the selection of appetizers and sides the client had chosen.

"We run out of notepads?" Kent turned the cardboard over to see it had come from a crate of plain Greek yogurt.

"Another thing I'm doing more of, recycling," Ernesto said proudly.

Kent chuckled and studied the list. Since he'd known his sous chef, the guy had gone through multiple phases, including several fad diets. Kent wasn't sure why, since he had a lean, muscular build and seemed to be able to eat anything he wanted.

"I'll get the ducks prepped and ready to go in the oven if you want to tackle the medallions," said Kent.

Ernesto nodded as he got up to wash his plate in the stainless-steel sink. "Ready when you are."

When her colleagues began leaving the lab, Susa sighed and checked the clock on the wall. Five o'clock. Time to go home and get dressed for the party. Last year she had forgotten all about the dinner and got a warning from her boss. If she wanted to get into management, he reminded her, she needed to attend functions like this.

As she drove home, Susa mentally reviewed the clothes in her closet. What was she going to wear? She felt that same panic she always got at having to dress for big social functions.

Forty-five minutes later, Susa parked at the Tipping Whale and got out, smoothing down the red skirt she'd found at the back of her closet and adjusting the white angora turtleneck. She hadn't worn the outfit for a few years, but it still fit and looked perfect for the holiday theme. Slamming her car door, she straightened her spine and took a deep breath as she walked across the lot. Social occasions always made her feel so awkward and nervous. Pulling open the large, glass door, she was met with tiny white lights strung in a crisscross pattern on the dining room ceiling and potted poinsettias on each table. A tall Christmas tree decorated with shiny glass balls sat in one corner. She plastered a smile on her face. This would be over before she knew it, she reassured herself.

"What did you tell him?"

"Nothing, I swear." Hermann was still dressed in his swim trunks, his blond, curly hair damp from the lake. They stood under the giant oak tree. Susa peered into the black summer night toward the road.

"He's just late," said Hermann. "We can always go see if he's working at the bowling alley tonight."

Susa shook her head vigorously. "Absolutely not. He'll think we're stalking him."

"He likes you, hon. Take it from me. He'd be thrilled if we went to the bowling alley."

"Do you really think so?"

"I know so. In the meantime, did you bring beer from your dad's stash?"

Susa pulled a Heineken out of her bag and handed it to Hermann.

"This is warm."

"So."

"No one drinks warm beer."

"Well, tonight you do." Susa peered into the darkness again, hoping, praying that Rogue would come.

5

"You okay?" Ernesto asked Kent when he saw him grasp his lower back.

"My back is just a little tight is all."

"If you need to sit down in the office, I can do the chef appearance."

"So that's what this is about. You want the limelight." Kent reached for his chef's hat. "Come out with me."

"Someone's gotta keep an eye on the food. Go razzle dazzle them. Juana says they're raving about the appetizers."

Kent smiled and headed for the kitchen's swinging doors. The lab party guests filled the main dining area. He had shut the restaurant down to other customers for the night. Kent scanned the two long tables, noting they were a rowdy bunch for scientists. He headed for the table closest to him, lightly putting his hands on the shoulders of a man and woman.

"How's the food so far?"

The woman looked up and smiled. "The poached pears with brie are my favorite. They're delicious. And your Christmas decorations are wonderful."

"I'm so glad to hear that."

Glancing over at the other table, he saw Juana handing a drink to a woman with red hair. He held his breath for a moment, like he always did whenever he saw a redhead, then reminded himself. There were millions of people in Southern California. The chances of running into her were slim to none. As if she could hear his thoughts, the woman looked up and right at Kent. *It was her.* When their eyes met, she appeared puzzled at the intensity of his stare, then broke eye contact and looked down at her plate.

After the waitress gave Susa her soda, she saw the chef looking her way. He had an odd expression on his face. Rather than continuing to meet his gaze, she felt her cheeks flush as she pulled her eyes away. Reaching for the breadbasket and taking out a roll, she stole a glance to see him still staring at her. Something about his gaze caused her heart to thrum in her chest. She took a drink of her soda as another man came out of the kitchen and said something to him.

"Are you thinking about your experiment again?" asked Bernard as she watched the chef go back into the kitchen. "We're supposed to be having a good time."

Susa kept her eyes on the swinging kitchen doors as she replied, "I am having a good time. Food's terrific." For once when it came to a social event, Susa was telling the truth. She felt her phone buzzing in her purse, but it could wait. Right now, she wanted to peek at her face to make sure she hadn't smeared her lipstick. Picking up her dessert spoon, she turned it over and surreptitiously checked.

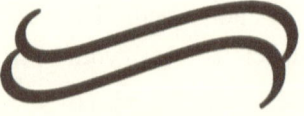

Kent struggled to hear what Ernesto was saying as his mind processed the fact that Susa sat yards away in the dining room.

"So, what do you want me to do?"

"Do?"

"I'm not sure what happened, but I don't think the balsamic reduction is going to be enough to compensate for the dryness of the pork."

Kent shook his head to clear it. "Serve the medallions with a gravy. Use the reduction to make it."

Ernesto nodded. "That's what I was thinking but wanted your okay." He went back to the stove while Kent checked the ducks in the oven. They looked ready. He pulled the giant pan out and pierced the birds with a meat thermometer. Perfect. He had soaked them in a salty brine, so he knew at least they wouldn't be dry.

Glancing at his wristwatch, he calculated. If Ernesto had the gravy done in five minutes, they'd still be pretty much on schedule. As he plated up the duck, Kent began to wonder. Maybe his eyes had been playing tricks on him. After all, how many times had he seen a redhead and thought it was Susa?

Susa felt the sting of disappointment when Hermann finally convinced her to go to the bowling alley to look for Rogue. He wasn't there. Instead, they found the owner spraying deodorizer into the shoes and fanning the aerosol spray out of his face.

"He didn't show up for work tonight," the owner told them. "And it's not the first time. I don't run no charity." He slammed down a pair of bowling shoes, making Susa jump. "I got a message for him when you see him. He's fired."

Susa had chosen the duck, and it was delicious. If she had the courage, she'd like to tell the chef how good it was, but he hadn't come back out into the dining room.

After dinner, the lab director made a speech and praised some of the researchers and their work over the past year. Susa was one of them.

"Teacher's pet," Bernard said when her name was mentioned.

Susa laughed, then noticed what looked like a flash of irritation in his eyes. Just then, the director welcomed them to enjoy dessert, and Susa thought about excusing herself. If she hurried home, she could go right to bed and get back into the lab early tomorrow morning before anyone came in. She was about to make her excuses when the chef and waitress came out of the kitchen with two large platters. The chef looked her way, and something shifted in Susa. She decided to stay for dessert.

Kent tried not to stare at Susa as he and Juana made their way out with the two platters of Baked Alaska. He set a cake at the head of Susa's table, stealing a glance at her as he pulled a knife out of his smock and set it on the table.

The man in charge, named Phillip, whispered to him. "We have some announcements to make. If you could serve while we're doing that, we'll stay on schedule."

Kent nodded and began cutting slices, making his way around the table as he offered up each plate. The closer he got to Susa, the more he searched for the words to say to her so that she might recognize him. When she looked up into his eyes as he asked if she wanted a slice, he saw curiosity on her face.

He opened his mouth to say something to her when Phillip stood and announced, "Thank you all for coming. I know it's been a long year, and this holiday dinner is a small token of our appreciation. I'm sure you would all have liked for the department to send you on a cruise, but the budget wouldn't allow it." The entire room laughed as Kent set down Susa's cake and moved on to the next person.

. . .

When the dinner came to a close, Susa glanced toward the kitchen doors. The chef hadn't come out since dessert. The odd thing was he seemed so familiar, and she wanted to catch a glimpse of him again. But when she looked into his face for that moment, he didn't really look like anyone she knew. Still, there was something about the eyes. As everyone was leaving, she took a minute to thank her boss for a lovely evening. Bernard offered to walk her to her car, but she told him she needed to use the restroom. When she came out a few minutes later, the room was nearly clear except for the server and busboy and a couple of her colleagues. She glanced at the kitchen doors, still wondering, then walked out into the night.

As the party wound down, Kent kept trying to get into the dining room again, but they were swamped in the kitchen. Susa might not remember him, but he couldn't just let her walk away without saying hi. When at last he made his way out of the kitchen, he was disappointed to see the room practically empty. A few people lingered, while Juana and Raul bussed the dirty dishes.

"You need something, boss?" Juana asked.

"There was a woman. Red hair. Did you see her leave?"

"Yeah, she just walked out."

Kent rushed through the front door and glanced both ways down the street. He saw her in the distance next to a parked car and called out, "Susa!"

She turned at the sound of her name and waited while he took long strides in her direction.

When they were a few feet apart, he saw her eyes widen. He stopped in front of her. "You do recognize me."

"Rogue?"

He chuckled. "No one has called me that for a long time. I go by my given name, Kent, nowadays. How have you been, Susa?"

She seemed lost for words and finally stammered, "I, you, what are you...?"

"Doing here? I opened the restaurant three years ago. I had no idea you worked at UCI."

"I had no idea either. I mean, that you were here."

Kent smiled, remembering how he'd always found Susa's unpretentiousness so attractive. "It probably took you off guard," he said.

"I had no idea. I have to admit, you don't look like I remember."

"There's reasons for that connected to my years as a race car driver. I'd be happy to explain them if you'd like to wait until after I've closed."

Susa opened her mouth to answer when someone wearing a ski mask came running from the street and pointed a gun at them. "Make one move, and I'll shoot you." It was a man's muffled voice.

"Hold on, buddy," said Kent, putting his arms up. "We'll give you whatever you want."

The man gestured to Susa. "She knows what we want. She just needs to hand it over."

Kent looked to Susa. Her eyes were filled with terror. "Do you know what he's talking about?" he asked.

She shook her head.

"You've got the wrong person," said Kent.

He saw a woman on the opposite side of the street approaching them. The man must have noticed, because his agitation rose. "Give me the bag now, or your boyfriend is going to die."

"I don't have it here," Susa said, to Kent's surprise. "Let him go. He has nothing to do with this."

Just then, the approaching woman must have spotted the man's gun, because she started screaming.

"Dammit," the man said, pushing Susa toward Kent and running down the street before disappearing into an alley.

27

When the masked man shoved Susa into Kent's arms, she was shaking so hard she stayed there, unable to step away.

"What's going on?" he asked.

"I have no idea who that man was."

"But you knew exactly what he wanted?" Concern lined Kent's handsome face.

Susa didn't speak.

"Let's get off the street and back into the restaurant," Kent suggested.

Once inside, he commented, "What a reunion." Kent cocked his head just like Susa remembered as he looked at her. Dishes clinked in the kitchen, and the restaurant's front lights had been dimmed. "White Christmas" played in the background, and the sparkly lights on the ceiling gave the room a soft glow.

"I'm really sorry about that outside." Then she glanced around the restaurant. "I never pegged you for a chef."

"As I mentioned before we were held at gunpoint, I was a race car driver for nine years before this. I quit after a bad crash that damaged my face." Kent's eyes seemed to pierce hers. "But I can tell you all about that once you tell me what's going on."

"It was a case of mistaken identity," said Susa, her worry rising about Hermann. Whatever her cousin had gotten involved in this time appeared to be more dangerous than she could have expected.

Kent came closer to her, until they were inches apart, his warm breath caressing her cheek. "You always were a terrible liar. The man said, give me the bag, and you told him you don't have it. What's going on? Tell me, maybe I can help you."

Susa let out an exasperated breath. "It's Hermann. You remember my cousin?"

"Anyone would remember Hermann. What does he have you involved with this time?"

Susa glanced at the restaurant's front door, then back at Kent. "I'm holding a bag of diamonds for him."

Kent believed Susa was telling the truth. It was Hermann he wasn't so sure about.

"Did he tell you whose diamonds they are?"

"No. He said someone dropped them off with him."

"The old, 'they're my friend's' routine?'"

"Something like that. He told me to put them in the lab. I think because it's a secure facility."

"Did you?"

Susa hesitated.

"Are they on you?"

"They're in my house. I can't be caught with potentially stolen goods at work."

Kent nodded. "I'd say there's no potentially about it. Where's your cousin now?"

"I'm not sure. He called me early this morning and sounded really vague." Questions formed in her eyes. "You're smiling."

"I am," Kent said. "I was just wondering what the odds are that we'd run into each other after all these years."

Susa's face colored an endearing shade of pink. "I'd say the odds are pretty slim," she said.

"It must be the destiny Hermann always talked about as he had us gaze up at the stars."

Susa laughed. "I guess so." Then her face took on a bewildered expression. "I really thought Hermann had cleaned up his act this last year. He met a guy named Brad and really appeared to be settling down. They were even talking about adopting a child."

Ernesto came out of the kitchen then. "All done, boss." He stopped short. "Sorry, I didn't know you were with someone."

"No worries. This is Susa. We met years ago in Georgia, if you can believe it. She works at UCI in the lab now. Susa, this is Ernesto, my sous chef and right-hand man."

Ernesto shook Susa's hand. "Very nice to meet you." Then he looked at Kent. "You lived in Georgia?"

"For a bit." He changed the subject. "Did Juana leave?"

"Yeah. I'm going home now, too. Nice to meet you again, Susa."

Once the front door shut, Kent asked her. "Would you like a drink?"

She shook her head. "I'm driving."

"It doesn't have to be alcohol. Don't you like 7-Up?"

Her eyes brightened. "You remember that?"

There are many things I remember, thought Kent, but instead he replied, "Of course. With a maraschino cherry."

"I'd love one."

Kent went behind the bar and motioned for Susa to sit down. He poured her soda, plunked in a cherry and handed her the glass, along with a straw. "So, tell me what you've been doing for the past twenty years."

"I got my master's in molecular biology and then my doctorate three years ago, and since then I've been studying plants to uncover information about human genomes."

"That sounds over my head, but fascinating," said Kent, pouring himself a whiskey neat.

This must be what floating feels like, thought Susa as she sipped her soda. Here she was talking with Kent. And he seemed genuinely interested in her and what she was doing.

"It is fascinating," she said. "I'm near a breakthrough right now, which is exciting."

Kent started to reply, when he heard a buzz. He pulled his phone out of his pocket and glanced at it. "Excuse me for a minute," he said. "Something I need to deal with."

Susa nodded as he texted, and her heart sank. Of course, he had a girlfriend. She was probably wondering where he was. She took a long drink of her soda.

When Kent finished and started to speak again, Susa interrupted. "I'm sure you have other things to do. It was very nice seeing you. I should get home now. I have an early morning tomorrow."

Kent looked surprised. "Let me walk you to your car. I'm concerned about whoever that was out in the street."

Susa stood and put her purse on her shoulder. "I'll get ahold of Hermann and tell him to take the bag back. My life and work are too important to me. Sorry to have put you in that position outside."

Concern filled Kent's eyes again.

"How about I give you my phone number, in case you need anything?"

She hesitated, then handed him her cellphone. "You can put your number in."

At her car a few minutes later, Kent touched her arm. "I meant it. Call or text me if you need anything."

I'm sure your girlfriend will love that, thought Susa, but she replied, "Okay. It was nice seeing you Rogue, I mean Kent."

"It was more than nice to see you, Susa. Keep in touch, okay?"

Susa gave him a quick hug, then, without meeting his eyes, got into her car and started the engine. As she drove down the street, she thought how seeing Kent again was the best part of the night.

"What is it, Hermann? Tell me."

They were sitting on the porch swing at her aunt's lake house. Her cousin looked beyond her eyes over her shoulder. "I saw Rogue with someone."

Susa felt tears forming at the back of her eyes. "Someone?"

"A girl, but it could have been his sister."

"What did she look like?"

Her cousin looked chagrined. "Blond, and let's just say, curvy." He stopped talking, and the Georgia night air felt like it had come to suffocate Susa.

"And beautiful? No freckles, right? Or long, gangly legs and a flat chest like me!"

"After this summer, you'll probably never see him again, anyway."

Susa willed the tears not to flow, but they slid down her cheeks, anyway. Hermann responded by pulling her close to him. "Aww, hon, this is your first summer romance. Believe me, it'll fade. You'll forget all about Rogue by homecoming."

Kent watched Susa's car head down MacArthur. He sure hoped she'd be okay. And he wondered what had ended their conversation so abruptly. Then it occurred to him. She might have someone at home. Here he was assuming she was single. Just his luck to finally find her and she's not available.

As Kent drove home, the more he thought about the thug on the street, the more nervous he got. By the time he pulled up in front of his house, he'd decided. A friend in the Santa Ana PD owed him.

8

When Susa pulled into her driveway, she turned off the car, sitting there for a moment as the engine settled. She had to call Hermann. After dialing his number, she heard his voicemail. Anxiety threaded its way up her back. It wasn't like Hermann to stay away from his phone for this long.

"Darn it, Hermann," she said to an empty car.

Getting out, she walked quickly to the front door, suddenly wondering if anyone was watching her. Nerves tight, she unlocked the door, then hurried inside and latched it shut. Slipping out of her high heels, she padded into the living room and noticed the curtains were still open from this morning, when she'd flung them wide to allow in sunlight for her houseplants. Without turning on the lights, she pulled the curtains closed, then peeked out onto the quiet street. Her heart beating louder than the grandmother clock ticking in the corner, Susa hoped she'd hear from Hermann in the morning with a perfectly reasonable explanation like he'd lost his phone or dropped it in water. As she headed to her bedroom to get ready for bed, she couldn't help but think of Rogue, whose real name appeared to be Kent. Where had he been all these years? Race car driving? She had so many questions.

Kent had gotten ahold of his friend Joey Landau, who talked to a source at the DMV and got Susa's address. She lived not far from the laboratory.

"Who is she to you?" asked Joey.

Kent and Joey had met when he raced. Joey had bet on the races, but at the time was doing more drinking than anything else. Kent brought him home to sober up on more than one occasion. He was glad to see that Joey was clean now.

"We met years ago in Georgia, if you can believe it. This whole thing involves her cousin. And I'm worried about her safety."

"Is her cousin bad news?"

"He'd never hurt her himself. But someone approached Susa near the restaurant tonight. He left when a bystander started making noise, but I'm afraid he might have followed her home."

"Why'd you let her head home alone?"

"She wanted to, so I figured she has someone there."

"Well, there's no other car registered to that address," said Joey. "Your friend could be all alone with her admirer right now."

"Shit. Can you do something about that?"

"I'm almost off duty. I'll stop by on my way home and check on her. And I'll let you know what happens."

"Thanks, I really appreciate it," said Kent, who realized he'd been anxious since Susa left his sight.

After a warm bubble bath, Susa toweled off, then reached for her robe and wrapped herself in it. She thought about Kent hugging her after the man had attacked and pulled her pink terrycloth robe tighter. Suddenly, her front doorbell rang. Susa pressed her lips together and held her breath as she walked quietly to the door, unsure of what to do next. If it was the man wanting the diamonds, what should she do?

"Susa York? Can you open up? I'm with the Santa Ana Police Department."

The lump in her throat turning to lead, Susa peered through the peephole. A dark-haired man wearing jeans and a t-shirt held up a badge. Steeling herself against bad news about Hermann, she opened the door a crack.

"Are you Susa York?"

"Yes."

"My friend Kent Aronson asked me to see if you're okay," he said. "I'm sorry if I alarmed you."

Susa opened the door wider. "You know Kent?"

The man nodded. "Is there anyone at home with you?"

"No."

"I'm just making sure you're safe and secure."

"Did he tell you about the man?" Susa asked in a low voice.

"He said someone accosted you in the street near his restaurant. I'm not on duty anymore tonight, but you can call me anytime." He handed her a card. Susa studied it for a moment.

"Kent's a good guy," said Joey.

"Thank you, Detective Landau."

He smiled. "Call me Joey. And I meant it when I said to call me." He surveyed the street and then glanced behind her in the house. "You sure you don't want me to check the place out?"

"I've been home for a while. I think it's okay, but thank you," said Susa.

"Okay," he said, turning to leave. "Lock up now."

Don't worry about that, thought Susa as she deadbolted the front door. When she was in the kitchen checking the lock on the bay window, she thought she saw a shadow move in the backyard. Her hands shaking, she turned off all the lights in the kitchen and peered out into the dark night. She didn't see anything again, even though she waited for a good minute, but she couldn't help having a dark feeling like someone was watching. Pulling Joey's card from her robe pocket, she held it tight as she went to her bedroom. Sliding off her robe, she put her cellphone and the card under her pillow and laid down.

9

When Kent heard from Joey that Susa was safely at home, he was relieved. He glanced at his phone for the umpteenth time. Only a message from his sister. He should return Gloria's call. She liked to check in with Kent at least once a week, but she was probably asleep by now.

Sleep was likely going to elude Kent again tonight. Ever since the race-track accident, he often had a hard time sleeping. Now worrying about Susa, he might as well give up getting any sleep.

Sliding open the door leading out onto his deck, he shivered as Southern California's brand of December chill rushed at him. The large thermometer on the side of the house read forty degrees. Pulling his tele-scope onto the deck, he checked the sky and focused on the three bright stars of Orion's Belt. As he admired the twinkling solar system, he thought about Susa all those summers ago under the moonlight. He was smitten from the first moment he laid eyes on her. Did she still look at the stars?

When Susa woke the next morning, she reached over to her night-stand for her phone. On the screen, she saw Kent's number in her contacts and wondered, where did he live? She hadn't given him a chance to tell her much. She thought about calling to tell him she was okay, but what would she say? Sorry to disturb you and your girlfriend? Susa got up and went to the kitchen to make herself some coffee. As she waited for it to brew, she looked out the bay window. In the early morning sun, she was relieved to see that nothing seemed out of place in the backyard. A house wren flew in front of the window for a moment, as if to say good morning, or more likely, feed me. They liked it when she sprinkled bird-seed on the grass.

When the coffee finished brewing, she pulled open a cupboard and took out a cup that said, "World's Best Aunt." She smiled at the thought of her nephew, Devan, with his impish grin. He loved spending time at Susa's. They'd have pillow fights and stay up late watching Disney movies. She spooned sugar into her coffee and stirred, then sat down at the kitchen table. No messages on her phone still. Hopefully Hermann was hard at work at the coffee shop and just hadn't had a chance to contact her. When the phone buzzed in her hand, she jumped. It was Brad, Hermann's boyfriend.

"Susa, have you heard from Hermann?"

Her pulse suddenly thundering in her ears, Susa sat up straight. "He's not with you?"

"I haven't seen him in a couple of days. I'm really worried. Have you talked to him recently?"

Susa was silent. Hermann had sworn her to secrecy about the diamonds.

"Susa, I can hear you breathing, so I know we didn't lose our connection. What aren't you telling me? Do you know where he is?" Brad's voice was strained.

"I don't know," said Susa, truthfully. "I heard from him two days ago, and I've been trying to get ahold of him ever since. I'm concerned now that I know he's not with you. I was hoping he was just busy."

"Should I report him missing?"

"That might be a good idea, Brad," Susa said softly. "Hermann doesn't keep people he loves worried. I know someone in the police department who may be able to help us. I'll call you back."

Susa dialed the number on Joey's card.

"Landau speaking."

"Hi, this is Susa, you came to my house last night?"

"You okay?"

"Yes, but I'm afraid something may have happened to my cousin. He's been missing for a couple of days. I can come down to the station with his partner. He may be able to give you more information."

"If you can get here within the hour, I'll be here."

When they walked into the station twenty minutes later, Susa wasn't sure if she or Brad was more nervous. Usually cracking jokes, her cousin's boyfriend appeared pale, his face drawn.

"What's your cousin's name?" asked Joey as he led them into the back.

"Hermann St. James," said Susa.

"When was the last time you were in contact with him?" Joey gestured for Susa and Brad to sit in the chairs across from him at a desk with his nameplate.

"He called me two nights ago," said Susa, who looked over at Brad.

"I saw him two days ago, in the morning. He was headed to work at the coffee shop. He was supposed to come home in the late afternoon, but he never showed up. At first, I thought he might have had to do a double shift."

Joey took down Hermann's age and weight and what he was wearing, then consulted his computer.

"Are you checking for unidentified bodies?" asked Brad, his voice cracking slightly.

Joey pulled his eyes away from the computer. "Yes, but no reports fitting his description. I'm also checking local hospitals." He looked back at the screen. "Nothing. Has he ever done anything like this before?"

"Never," said Brad. "I just know something is really wrong."

Susa shifted in her seat and glanced across the room. She thought about how she and Hermann always kept each other's secrets. But he was missing, and Kent trusted Joey. She gave Brad a sidelong glance, then met Joey's eyes. "My cousin has a bit of a checkered past."

"Go on," said Joey.

"Yeah, go on," said Brad. "This is news to me."

Susa took a deep breath. "Brad, Hermann didn't want you to ever know about this, but I think it's important to mention. He used to smuggle...stolen goods."

Brad looked shocked.

"What kind of stolen goods?" asked Joey.

Susa turned to Brad. "I want you to know that he got out of the business when he met you. He's been doing really good, which is why I'm so worried."

"Just spit it out, already, Susa," said Brad. "What did he smuggle?"

"Gems and fine art. And," Susa cleared her throat, "before he disappeared, Hermann left me with a bag of purple diamonds."

10

"This changes everything," said Joey. "Where are the diamonds?"

"At my house. He wanted me to store them at work, but I couldn't chance getting caught with them. It could ruin my funding." She hesitated and reddened. "I guess now I'm technically caught with them."

"Don't worry about that. You said they're purple?"

"Many of them, yes."

"Purple diamonds are some of the rarest in the world. They're likely worth a fortune." Joey ran his hands through his hair. "I worked a case awhile back involving a missing purple diamond. That one was worth nearly a million dollars."

Susa sucked in her breath. "Oh, my god. I had no idea that was even possible."

"And nothing from Hermann." Joey seemed to be talking to himself now.

Susa shook her head, worry settling in her chest.

"He could just be hiding out until the heat is off," Joey said. "How about we go to your house. I'll bring the diamonds back to the station as evidence."

"That sounds good," said Susa. Now that she knew how much the diamonds might be worth, she welcomed getting them out of her house.

"We'll have them checked out by a gemologist to make sure." Joey stood and took his gun out of his desk drawer, sliding it into a holster.

"What should I do?" asked Brad, who remained sitting, his hands glued to the chair.

"Keep your phone on at all times in case he contacts you."

"I've known Hermann my whole life," Susa said quietly, putting her hand on Brad's tense shoulder. "He always lands on his feet."

"Keep reminding me of that," said Brad.

Brad decided to go home in case Hermann showed up there, and Joey followed Susa to her house. When they arrived and she got out of the car, he stopped her from walking to the front door.

"It doesn't look like anyone is here but let me go ahead of you to make sure." He put his hand out for the key.

Joey opened the front door, and had Susa stay out front. A few minutes later, he told her to come in and shut the door.

"The diamonds are here in the living room," said Susa, walking over to the bookcase and kneeling to reach behind her molecular biology book. She grabbed the bag and pulled it out, standing up and handing it to Joey. He undid the drawstring and peered inside. Pulling out a purple diamond, he made a low whistle as he held it up to the light.

"I'd say these are the real deal." He met Susa's gaze. "Is there anything you didn't tell me yet? Anything about your cousin you didn't want Brad to know?"

His question took Susa by surprise. "Like he's leading a double life?"

"Anything like that."

"No, he really was trying to walk the straight and narrow. And there's no one else. He is crazy about Brad." Susa thought about recently shopping with Hermann for Brad's Christmas gift, a gold band meant to be a proposal.

Joey put the bag of diamonds in an envelope marked evidence. "Is there anywhere else you can stay?"

"Not really. My sister lives in Irvine, but she has a son and husband, and her house is small. With the holiday, she has a lot going on."

Joey glanced around her living room. "I'd feel a lot better if you weren't here. What about Kent's place?"

At his words, Susa felt a fluttery sensation in her stomach. "Kent and I, we don't know each other that well. I mean, it was a long time ago when we knew each other."

"Okay, well you've got my number. Anything suspicious at all, you give me a call, okay?"

"I promise," said Susa.

After Kent hung up with Joey, he scribbled Susa's address on a napkin and considered his next move. Joey had made it clear that Susa appeared to be alone, and that really bothered Kent. But how to tell her that? He didn't want her to think he was being too familiar. They'd only just reunited after two decades of living their individual lives. Maybe he'd stop by her house tonight after work to check up on her.

By the time the dinner hour had come and gone, and the restaurant's kitchen was cleaned, and the next day's prep completed, it was nearly eleven o'clock. Too late, Kent decided, to go knocking on Susa's door.

Susa stretched her neck and checked the time. It was after eleven. She had gone to the lab after giving Joey the diamonds to get a few hours of work in, but now her stomach growled, and her eyes were tired. She shut off her equipment and signed out.

When she pulled in front of her house a few minutes later, Susa saw that the blinds in the front room were drawn closed. She felt the hairs on her arms tingle. She always left them open during the day for her house-plants, especially her bonsai.

Heart in her throat, she began digging in her purse for Joey's card, but she couldn't find it. She must have left it in the lab. Fingers shaking, she unlocked her phone and dialed Kent's number. He picked up imme-diately.

"Hello?"

"So sorry to bother you, Kent, but there might be someone in my house."

"Susa? Where are you?"

"In front of my house, in my car. I just got home."

"Don't go in. Did you call Joey?"

"I can't find his card."

"I'll call him. Leave right now and come to the restaurant."

As Susa drove away, her arms shook on the wheel. It looked like this time Hermann had gotten in way over his head.

When she pulled in front of the restaurant, Kent was standing outside. Relief washed through her to see him as she lowered her driver's side window.

He put his hands on the door and leaned toward her. "Joey's going to check out your house. Want to come inside while we wait?"

Susa nodded.

He stood beside her door. "You'll want to shut off your car engine then." Kent smiled slightly.

Susa laughed as she turned off her car, and Kent opened the door for her.

"Did you eat?" he asked once he'd ushered her inside and locked the door.

"Actually, I'm famished. I was just about to go in my house and eat a peanut butter sandwich."

"Fine dining." Kent grinned, making Susa feel awkward. Why did she tell a chef she was going to eat a peanut butter sandwich?

"It's okay," he said. "I like peanut butter and jelly sandwiches."

"Actually, it was going to be a peanut butter and honey sandwich."

"Even better." His eyes twinkled. Was he making fun of her? Noticing her discomfort, he came toward her and put his hands on her shoulders. "Hermann can take care of himself. He's going to be okay." Susa nodded.

"How about I make you a Portobello burger?"

Susa swore her legs had turned into jelly. She knew she should be worrying about Hermann, but right now with Kent's eyes on hers and his hands sending tingles throughout her body, she couldn't even think.

Kent's phone buzzed, and he checked the screen. "It's Joey," he said, and answered it.

"Anything?"

Kent listened for a few moments, then hung up.

"Your place was ransacked."

11

Stunned, Susa couldn't speak.

"This might be stating the obvious, but you can't stay at your house until this is all figured out," said Kent.

"I'll have to check into a hotel."

"Nonsense. You can stay with me."

Susa eyed him dubiously. "Are you sure?"

"I'm positive, and I won't have it any other way. You'll be out of danger there." What he didn't add was that he could keep his eye on her.

"Where is your home?"

"Trabuco Canyon. It's a very special area, scenic and peaceful."

"Think it's safe to stop at my house first?"

"If we make it quick."

Susa gasped at the wreckage in her living room. The coffee table was on its side, and her books were strewn all over the floor. She picked up the molecular biology book, thinking how close whoever ransacked her house came to finding the diamonds. She set the book next to the front door with her bonsai tree, which fortunately came out unscathed. Then she went upstairs to pack a bag.

Kent checked out the living room, amazed at how thoroughly they seemed to have upturned every inch of the house. He picked up a photo of Susa and Hermann from the floor. They stood in front of a tree, Susa smiling into the camera with a carefree expression, while Hermann looked like he was plotting something.

"I love that photo," said Susa, who had snuck up behind him. She smelled like he remembered—lavender and sunshine.

"It's a good one." Kent handed the picture to her, and she slipped it into her suitcase.

As they walked to the car, Kent gingerly carried the bonsai after Susa told him how sensitive it was. "Does he need a seatbelt, do you think?" he asked jokingly as he set the plant on the passenger seat.

Susa put the key in her ignition. "I'll follow you, so don't go speeding off."

He eyed her hybrid car and chuckled. "My Miata could easily leave this little thing in the dust."

As they headed toward Trabuco Canyon, Kent thought about how after twenty years of wondering what happened to Susa, she was coming home with him.

"Why do we have to leave? I like it here. I've got friends." Kent pouted.

"I need to go where the work is. There's a lot of waitressing jobs in Atlanta. Two weeks from now when the summer visitors start to leave, it's going to be dead here at the yacht club. Go on and pack up. I want to get on the road tonight."

Kent knew better than to argue with his sister. He wondered if he should give notice at the bowling alley, but he had to be careful in case someone called Social Services on them. Better not to take a chance and risk things.

He hated leaving Susa and Hermann. They were supposed to meet under the oak tree again tonight. He didn't have time to find them, though. Instead, when the moon was high that night, Kent was pulling up at a motel fifty miles away.

How much did Susa remember about that summer at the lake? Kent wondered as he pulled onto the gravel drive that led to his house. It was probably something she took for granted, since she went every summer, but Kent remembered every detail of what he often considered the best summer of his life.

When they emerged from their respective cars and shut the doors, the stillness of the night settled around them. It was always this way out here. So hushed was the forest surrounding his house that Kent would always stop and allow the quiet to seep into him.

Susa gazed at the moonlit sky. "It's beautiful. And so quiet. I feel like I need to whisper."

Kent's shoes crunched on the dry brush covering the driveway as he came up next to her. "The quiet is my favorite part of living out here," he said. "That and the great views. Wait until you see it in the morning." She continued to look up at the sky, and Kent was reminded of the hitch in his chest he'd gotten each time he'd seen her that summer by the oak tree.

She turned to face him. "I don't want to put you in danger, Kent. The cloak and dagger routine was okay when we were kids, but this is…." She trailed off.

"Real?" Kent could sense fear and worry in Susa's voice. "I'm happy to have you here. Of course, it would be great if it was under better circumstances, but I'm sure the thing with Hermann will get worked out soon."

"He's a pain in the butt, but he means a lot to me."

"I know. How about we go inside?" He reached out and took her suitcase from her grasp. "You can carry in your tree."

"Your house has a cabin vibe," said Susa as they entered and stopped in a tiny entryway. "Like we're in the mountains."

"That was the main reason I decided to move in here. It reminded me of where I grew up."

"Where did you grow up?"

"The Ozarks, Georgia, and a few other places." Kent flicked a light switch, illuminating the living room. "You can put your tree on the coffee table, if you want. As you can see, the place is small. There's also the kitchen, and a bathroom and bedroom in the back. I can sleep on the couch, and you can take my bed."

"Oh, no, I couldn't do that. I'm putting you out enough as it is. I'll sleep on the couch." Susa looked around. "So, you're the only one who lives here?"

Kent's eyebrows shot up. "Who else would be living here?"

"Maybe a pet?"

He grinned. "Or are you asking if I have a girlfriend?" He suppressed the urge to laugh as Susa's cheeks turned scarlet.

"Oh, my god, no, I wouldn't ask you that. It's none of my business."

"It would become your business if my wife happened to walk in."

"You're married?" gasped Susa.

Kent had to admit the sound of disappointment in her voice made him happy.

"No, I'm not married, and I don't have a girlfriend, either."

Susa looked relieved. "Oh, good. I mean, I'm glad I won't be disturbing anyone."

"What about you?"

"What about me?"

"Is there someone who might come banging on my door ready to cart you off? Not counting whoever wants those diamonds."

"No, no one."

"Well, now that we've got that all settled, I'm going to make something to eat. I never made you that mushroom burger, and I'm starving."

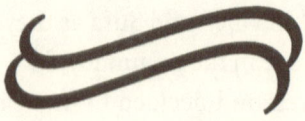

Susa watched as Kent went into the kitchen and opened the refrigerator. She was tempted to slap herself, just to make sure this was real. After all the times she dreamed about seeing Kent again, here she was, standing in his living room.

After a tasty meal of eggs, fried potatoes and fresh tomatoes, Kent yawned.

"You're probably tired after such a long day," said Susa. "Don't let me keep you up."

Kent put the dishes in the sink. "I am pretty beat. You going to be okay?"

"I'll be fine. Go to bed. You cooked. I'll wash the dishes."

As she began cleaning their plates, out of the corner of her eye, she saw Kent open a hallway cupboard and pull out a blanket and a pillow. He tossed them on the couch. "Help yourself to whatever you like," he said. "There's some drinks in the fridge. I'll check in with Joey first thing in the morning."

When Kent went into the bathroom and shut the door, Susa finished up the dishes and sat down on the comfy brown leather couch. On the coffee table sat a large wooden bowl piled high with pinecones she imagined he gathered from the forest. Probably his take on holiday décor, she smiled to herself. She pulled her microbiology textbook out of her suitcase and flipped it open, but after a few minutes, she realized she hadn't read a word.

12

The next morning, Susa awoke to the sound of a dove cooing outside the living room's bay window. She got off the sofa and crept over to get a closer look. The bird sat on a branch of live oak that shaded this side of the house. To her surprise, the dove stayed put and stared at her with his gray eyes. "Good morning, Mr. Dove," she said quietly, putting her hand on the glass as if to salute him.

"I see you met my resident dove."

Susa twirled around to find Kent standing behind her.

"Sorry to startle you."

Chest bare, he wore drawstring pajama bottoms. She noted a scar traveling from his breastbone down the length of his torso.

He must have seen her eyes on the scar, because he said, "The dangers of race-car driving, and the reason I'm now a chef. The damage to my face was more superficial and easier for the doctors to fix."

Susa had an overwhelming urge to run her finger over the scar to comfort him. She swallowed. "How bad was it? The crash?"

Pain seemed to fill his eyes for a moment. "Fiery. Bloody." Then he smiled. "But it's over now, and here we are."

"Yes, here we are." Susa glanced down at her bare feet. She didn't have any polish on her toes. Now she wished she'd taken her sister up on one of her many offers to get pedicures together.

Kent cleared his throat, and Susa responded by looking up at him, willing herself not to blush again.

"How about some eggs and coffee?"

"Sounds wonderful. I'll get dressed for work."

"Susa, you can't go into work today."

"But I have to. I have an experiment I need to check on."

"Can't one of your colleagues do that?"

"Not really. My colleagues have their own experiments to do."

"Okay, I'll go in with you while you check on things."

"You can't get into the lab. You're not authorized." Susa suddenly felt like a preschooler needing a chaperone. "I'll be fine. The lab is secure. And I don't have the diamonds, anyway." She picked up her suitcase and headed to the bathroom with it.

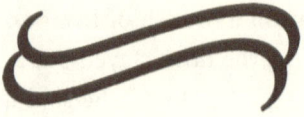

Kent sighed as he watched Susa go into the bathroom, clutching her suitcase. He went to retrieve his phone from the charger, checking the screen. Nothing from Joey, so he called him.

"No word on where your friend's cousin is, but I did find some inter-esting information," said Joey. "There's a German designer in LA's jewelry district who had a recent break-in, but he didn't report it. He's known to use a lot of the purple diamonds, which by the way are extremely rare."

"That's odd."

"This whole thing smells odd. We're talking about some major money here."

"Susa is dead set on going into work today."

"That seems kind of chancy, but she might be better off in the lab, since it's a secure building," said Joey.

"That's what she said, but I worry about her. You've heard of scientists that get really focused on their work. That's Susa."

Susa had left her hairbrush on the coffee table and opened the bathroom door to get it when she heard Kent talking on his cellphone. At the scientist reference, her heart fell. She closed the bathroom door and sat down on the toilet lid, pressing her fingers into her eyes to keep from crying. Once she could be certain of no waterworks, she cleaned her face and brushed her teeth.

When she exited the bathroom, Kent had two steaming plates of eggs on the table, along with mugs of coffee.

"Dig in," he said.

Susa had lost her appetite. Her first instinct was to leave, but he'd gone to all this trouble, so she decided to try and eat.

"You okay?" Ken had a concerned look on his face.

"Yes, just worried about Hermann. Thank you for breakfast."

"I talked to Joey. No word on Hermann, but there is a German jewelry designer in LA who had some diamonds taken from him."

Susa nodded. "I pray Hermann shows up soon." She ate her eggs as quickly as possible and took several cautious sips of her hot coffee. "Thank you for your hospitality." She got up and motioned to pick up her plate, but Kent stopped her, placing his hand on her arm.

"I'll clean up. Are you sure you're okay?"

Susa kept her eyes trained on her plate. "I'm an overfocused scientist. I'm always okay." She pulled her arm away and went to collect her things.

"Shit, Susa, you're taking what I said out of context. I was just trying to explain to Joey how worried I am about you."

"I'll be fine," Susa announced, eyes watery as she looked past Kent to the bay window. She noted the dove had flown away. Then she turned and marched out the door before she made a fool of herself with either tears or anger. After running down the front steps, she opened the car door, jumped in, and drove away.

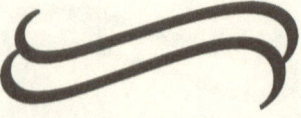

Kent stood on the front porch and watched Susa leave, angry with himself for his stupid choice of words. Besides making her feel bad, now she would probably never want to talk to him again. He went back into the house and slammed the door, his eyes falling on her little tree. Sitting down on the couch, he picked up the potted plant, turning it around in the morning light. The tree trunk was gnarled like an old man's arms, and the leaves were tiny. He let out a breath. At least he had an excuse to show up at the lab.

13

When Susa arrived at the lab, she found Bernard in her workspace. He heard her approaching and spun around. "Hey, I thought I left my pen here when we were talking yesterday, but I don't see it."

Susa put her purse down next to her microscope. "Next time just ask me. I'll take a look."

Bernard retreated to his workstation and Susa immediately felt badly about being short with him. She pulled her notebook from the drawer and began flipping through the pages of observational data she had recorded over the last few days.

As Susa dug into her research, all other thoughts slipped away. She spent the next several hours studying her findings and adjusting her calculations, all the while getting more excited. She was on the verge of a breakthrough; she just knew it. There was one more test to do. She needed to track down some oleander and jimsonweed for her study, both of which she could find in the wild. As she was gathering her things to leave the lab, her phone buzzed. A text message from Kent. *I'm really sorry, Susa. Please stay safe.*

"That's the tenth time I've seen you check your phone in the last five minutes. What's up?"

Kent and Ernesto stood at the butcher block counter in the restaurant's kitchen going over the order list for the week.

"It's Susa."

"What's up? Things seemed tense last night when she came in at closing."

"Long story, but someone ransacked her house. She's in trouble because of her cousin."

"Sounds like my family."

"She spent last night at my place, since hers isn't safe anymore."

"I would think that would be good news." Ernesto grinned.

"It was until I opened my big mouth this morning." Kent cringed at the memory. "I was talking to my cop friend and mentioned that she was an overfocused scientist. She overheard."

Ernesto whistled. "Bet that broke the mood."

"Now she's livid with me. She won't answer my texts."

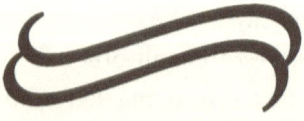

Susa drove into the parking lot at Irvine Park and stopped the car. She pulled a specimen bag out of her glove compartment and rubber gloves. Jimsonweed caused hallucinations, so she had to be ultra-careful not to get the plant sap on her skin where it could make its way into her system. Her phone buzzed. Kent again, asking how she was doing. She replied, *Doing great. Very busy.* Then she hit send. Susa got out of the car and headed for the lake in the center of the park. As she walked, she shook the vision of Kent bare-chested in his pajama bottoms out of her head and reminded herself of his impression of her. Then she thought of her cousin and how badly she wished things were back to normal and he would answer his phone and give her some good brotherly advice.

"That's Rogue's sister?"

"Looks that way," said Hermann. They'd come to the bowling alley to wait for Rogue to finish for the night, so they could all go hang out at the lake. She and Hermann were sitting in the snack area eating fries when a young woman with dark hair came in. She and Rogue were talking, and then she glanced their way. Even her smile looked like Rogue's. She gave him a quick hug and left.

"She's not blond and curvy," said Susa.

"Hon, I'm telling you he likes you. I'm going to leave you two alone tonight."

"Hermann, please, don't. Promise me you won't leave me alone with him."

Her cousin rolled his eyes. "I promise, unless I have to take a whiz. Or did you want to come with for that?"

"Ha ha," said Susa, looking over at Rogue, who smiled and waved at her.

"I don't see him waving at any of the other girls in the bowling alley."

Susa stuck a mouthful of French fries in her mouth.

"Nothing to say when you know I'm right."

It wasn't long before Susa found the small path into a stand of trees where she'd seen the jimsonweed a few months ago. She would have taken the sample then, but she wasn't ready for it yet. Better to have it fresh. When she saw the telltale foliage and trumpet-shaped white flowers, she smiled in satisfaction. Taking out her collection kit, she removed the gloves and pulled them on. Slowly, she cut off a good piece of plant, including the blooming flower and another that had gone to seed. She put it all in the bag, then rolled off the gloves and deposited them in the bag and sealed it. Putting it all in her purse, she noticed the winter afternoon light waning. Probably best to head back to her car and get the specimen to the lab. She'd find oleander another day.

When she arrived at her car, there was a man leaning against the driver's side door. She glanced around the parking lot but saw no one else. Her heart thudding in her temples, she stopped several yards away and asked, "Who are you?"

The man rubbed a hand over his goatee, pulling his cap down on his head and answered in a Southern drawl, "I believe the question should be, how can I get Hermann back?"

"Where's my cousin?" Susa's breathing became shallow.

The man took a step toward her. "Tell me where the bag is, then we'll talk about your cousin." Susa turned to run, but he grasped her by the hair and yanked her back against him. "I don't want to hurt those pretty red curls." He breathed in her ear. "You take me to where the diamonds are, and we can get Hermann."

Susa struggled to free herself, but that caused him to hold her even tighter. "We can make this real gentle or real hard, it's up to you." The man's tone became steelier.

"I don't have the bag," she said. "I swear. You searched my house."

"But you know where the bag is."

Susa was silent.

"That's what I thought. Here's what we're goin' to do."

14

Kent stood outside the UCI laboratory a little before five, resolved to tell Susa how he really felt about her. Even if she didn't feel the same, she had to know he'd been thinking about her all these years. He leaned against the wall, hoping every time the door opened that she'd come walking out. Finally, a tall guy he recognized from the night before emerged.

"Excuse me, do you know Susa?"

The guy gave Kent a suspicious look. "Who are you?"

"A friend of hers. I'm also the chef at the Tipping Whale. I saw you sitting next to her last night at your holiday dinner."

Recognition flashed across the man's face. "Yes, I work with her."

"Is she still inside? I have something I need to tell her."

"No, she left all of the sudden this afternoon. Didn't say anything. Why?"

"Nothing important," said Kent, deciding not to alarm her coworker. "I'll catch up with her." He headed for his Miata, unsure of what to do next. Maybe he could find her at home.

"Where are you taking me?" The man had thrown Susa into the passenger seat of a beat-up Chevy truck and was heading out of the parking lot.

He glanced at her out of the corner of his eye, and a cold chill settled at the bottom of her stomach. "Don't say anything else, unless it's where the diamonds are. And make yourself useful. Get me a beer out of that cooler."

Susa pulled out a beer from a cooler at her feet and handed it to him. He took his right hand off the steering wheel and slammed the head of the bottle on the dashboard, knocking off the cap. Then he took a long pull and ran a sleeved arm across his mouth. He put the beer between his legs as he sped up the car. Susa's mind whirled as the daylight swiftly disappeared. If she told him the truth—that the bag was at police head-quarters—he might kill her. She was safest if he thought she had access to the diamonds. By the time he pulled off the road at a rest stop, the beginnings of a plan brewed in her mind.

Kent found Susa's house dark and pounded on the door. No sign of her car. He pressed Joey's number and waited.

"Landau."

"Susa's missing."

"I thought she was going to the lab?"

"I went there after work, but she wasn't there. Now I'm at her house, and there's no sign she's been here."

"Maybe she went to a relative's house?"

"She has a sister around here somewhere, but I don't know where. Can you track her phone? Find out where she is?"

"I already messaged our tech department. We should know momen-tarily where her phone is. I'm sure there's a perfectly good explanation."

Kent paced in front of Susa's front door as he waited, his heart dropping when he heard Joey cuss. "What is it?"

"According to GPS, her phone is at a rest stop off Peter's Canyon Road. Near Irvine Park. Any idea what she'd be doing out there?"

Kent kicked her screen door. This was all his fault. If he hadn't upset her.

"You freaking out isn't going to help the situation," said Joey. "I'm heading to the rest stop now."

"Give me the coordinates."

"You're a civilian. Leave this to me."

"Give me the damn coordinates."

Kent punched the rest stop coordinates into his GPS and tore out of Susa's driveway. It would take him about fifteen minutes to get there, if he broke the speed limit.

When the man stopped the car, he instructed Susa, "We're going to sit at the picnic table over there. Get me another beer. And get one for yourself. I want to loosen up that tongue of yours."

She was about to refuse the beer but changed her mind and reached in for another one. He grabbed both bottles from her grasp. When Susa motioned to get her purse, he stopped her. "Leave your bag here. Give me your phone."

Susa took out her cell and handed it to him. While he focused on turning off her phone, she reached into her purse and grabbed the plant collection bag, stuffing it into her coat pocket.

He threw the phone down on the seat. "Let's go."

They walked over to a picnic bench, and he directed her to sit down. "What's your name?" she asked as she sat.

He stayed standing and shrugged. "Call me Willie." He opened one of the beer bottles on the edge of the picnic bench and took a drink, then uncapped one for her.

"Who do you work for?" asked Susa.

"How do you know I work for someone?"

"This seems like a big operation, considering how much those diamonds are worth."

He grinned. "So, you do know what's at stake here. I work for someone mighty powerful. And he ain't going to take no for an answer. You best give me the information I need, and we'll all be happy."

"You need to tell me where Hermann is."

"They'll release him when we have the diamonds."

"In my purse. I've got the address where the diamonds are located. In a notebook."

His eyes narrowed. "You better not be messing with me, little lady. Stay here." He took a swig of his beer, then slammed it down on the picnic table and stalked off to the car.

Working quickly, Susa opened the bag of jimsonweed and put on the gloves, extracting the flower that had gone to seed. She pulled out several seeds and poured them into the neck of his beer, crushing them as she did so. Then she poured some of her beer on top, to wash the seeds into the depths of the bottle and tore off the gloves, cramming everything into her pocket.

He came back and dumped her purse on the table. "Hurry up."

Susa took a drink of her beer before opening her bag. "This is good." She held up the bottle to read the label.

"You're stalling. Find the address." He put his own bottle to his lips and seemed to finish it off.

Susa pretended to search around in her purse and prayed that the jimsonweed was fast acting, but she wasn't sure what would happen when mixed with beer.

"I'm having a hard time seeing in my purse. The lighting is bad out here."

The man cussed under his breath and turned on his cellphone flashlight, then came around behind her and shined it on the contents of her bag. Working slowly and methodically, she dug around until she found a small notebook. "It's in here," she said, pulling it out and opening it. When she did so, the light from his cellphone began to sway. She held her breath and peeked up at him. He had a strange look on his face. "Can you shine the light on the book?"

"I am," he slurred. Then a bat swooped close overhead, and he stumbled back and yelled. "What the hell was that?"

Susa stood, putting distance between herself and him by backing her way toward the other side of the table. "It's just a bat," she said. "There's a lot of them out here. Although, they do carry rabies, so you don't want one to bite you."

"Make them go away." Now, he was clearly seeing things. His head swiveled about as he batted the air, and he appeared panicked.

"The bats only get worse as the night goes on. How about we leave? I can drive," she suggested.

He struggled to pull himself together. "You're trying to trick me," he cried, rage morphing his face as he started to come around the table toward her, but began weaving and stumbling, instead. Then he started howling and punching the air in front of him.

Susa considered her next move. Getting the keys and taking off without him seemed like her best move. But how?

15

When Kent drove into the rest stop, his lights flashed over a man and Susa at a picnic bench. No sign of Joey. Stopping his Miata, he sprang out of the car and sprinted toward them.

"Look, it's a man to get rid of the bats!" Susa yelled.

"Susa, it's me, Kent." What the hell was she talking about?

The man turned around. "Are you the batman?" He looked half-crazed.

"Yeah, Susa's friend," Kent said soothingly, slowly moving toward the man. When he was a couple of feet away, he lunged at him, pushing the man down on the hard ground and landing on top of him. The man thrashed and screamed, but Kent hit him across the jaw, seeming to daze him. As Kent held his arms down, sirens sounded in the distance. "That must be Joey. Are you okay?" he asked Susa.

"I'm fine. He's going to be unpredictable. He ingested jimsonweed."

As if on cue, the man started howling and tried to bite Kent's arm. He bore down on him harder as a car pulled up. Joey came rushing over.

The man began yelling about bats attacking him as Kent got off him and Joey took over and cuffed him. "He ate some jimsonweed," Kent said. Then his eyes went to Susa. "I guess being a botanist has its perks."

Joey threw Willie in the back of his unmarked car, then turned to them. "I'll have our doctor look at him. Once he comes down, we can talk to him. I'll be in touch."

As Joey drove away, Kent pulled her to him. He felt her body shaking against his. When her shivering finally subsided, he pulled back and met her eyes in the dim light.

"Not bad for an overfocused scientist," she said quietly.

"Susa, I'm so sorry you heard that." He saw tears glisten in her eyes. "I only meant that you're not as worldly as some people." Oh, hell, he was really screwing this up.

"I get it," Susa said, pulling away from him and wiping her face with her coat sleeve. "I've never been as sophisticated as other women. I like things like microscopes and the fact that ferns are the only plants in the world that don't have flowers or seeds but reproduce by spores. I'm just me. Can you please take me home?" The pain in her eyes was palpable.

"Susa, I've never met anyone like you. And I'm not taking you home. You need to come home with me until I know you're safe."

She seemed to consider his words.

"I'm not just saying this to make you feel better." He moved closer to her, relieved that she didn't try to step back. Putting his hand under her chin, he drew her lips to his and kissed her, slow and deep and steady. She responded by wrapping her arms around him and returning the kiss, and all his senses erupted. When they finished, he saw a small smile on Susa's lips. "I've wanted to do that since the moment I met you," said Kent.

When they arrived at Kent's house, Susa suddenly felt exhausted. She sat down on the couch, while any remaining energy she had drained away.

Kent got her a glass of water. "Adrenaline wearing off?" He sat down next to her.

"I think so," said Susa.

"That used to happen to me after a race. I'd be flying high for a while after, then a big crash. If you want to sleep, go ahead." He motioned to get up, but Susa put her hand on his arm.

"Thank you for coming to get me," she said. "I don't even want to think about what could have happened if you didn't."

"Looked to me like you had things pretty well under control," said Kent. "You mean a lot to me, Susa." He kissed her forehead, and guided her to lay back on the couch, covering her with a blanket. Within moments, she felt herself drifting off to sleep.

When Susa awoke, she got up and went to the kitchen, flipping on the light and checking the clock on the microwave. Three am. She'd been sleeping for several hours. As quietly as possible, she opened the refrigerator. Kent had put a plate of pork chops, scalloped potatoes and broccoli on the top shelf. She smiled and set it in the microwave, turning it on for a minute. As she waited, she noticed a photo attached to the refrigerator of him standing in front of a race car. He held a helmet in his hands and wore a broad smile on his face. This was the face she remembered from all those years ago. If it was possible, he was even more handsome now.

The food was delicious from the first bite to the last. Once she finished, she put the dish in the sink, then went back to the couch. She should try to sleep again, but she just wasn't tired. Then she heard Kent cry out "no" several times from the bedroom. He sounded distressed. Susa got up off the couch and walked down the hallway. She hesitated, then tiptoed into the room. Stopping to stand over the bed, she watched as his face contorted with the dream. Kneeling beside the bed, she debated. If she touched him, he might startle. Finally, she said in a soothing tone, "Shh, it's okay."

Kent opened his eyes and saw her, surprise registering in them. "Are you okay?"

"I'm fine, but you were having a bad dream."

Kent ran his hands over his face. "I'm sorry I woke you up."

"You didn't. I woke up a while ago and ate the pork chops. I can't believe I slept through your cooking." Susa laughed. "I'm beginning to think that the fumes from the jimsonweed must have affected me."

"Lie down with me," said Kent, folding the covers back.

Susa wasn't sure if she heard him right. "What did you say?"

16

Kent's request sent a ripple of excitement throughout Susa. How many times had she longed, without realizing it, for him to want her?

Susa stayed next to the bed, her eyes falling on the muscled surface of Kent's bare chest. Should she take off her clothes? She didn't know for certain what he was asking. As she remained immobile, Kent sat up, swinging his legs over the side of the bed. Reaching out, he guided her to her knees and undid the buttons on her blouse, all the while keeping her gaze. He pushed the blouse off her shoulders and onto the floor behind her, then unclasped her bra. Susa sucked in her breath. Taking her breasts in his hands, he gently caressed them, and she felt her nipples harden. Smiling, he leaned down and took one breast in his mouth, then the other. By this point, everything in Susa longed for him. After some minutes, he motioned for her to stand up. She did as he wanted, silent. He unzipped her pants, pushing them down her legs, kissing her thighs as he did so. She stepped out of them and kicked them to the side.

"Take off your panties," he whispered, and watched her until she stood naked in front of him, her long ringlets laying over her aroused breasts. Kent pulled her close and took Susa by surprise when he buried his mouth between her legs, his tongue exploring the warm softness of her.

At the feel of his mouth, she closed her eyes, lips parted. Her body and mind reacted to him in a way she'd never experienced with any other man, and her knees grew weak. Then he pulled her back toward the bed with him, and when she laid down, he ran his hands the full length of her body, exploring and loving her.

"I can't tell you how often I've imagined this," he said, his voice soft as he nuzzled against her neck.

Susa started to speak, but he laid a finger over her lips. Then he kneeled on the bed and removed his pajama bottoms as Susa's heart began to thunder at the sight of him. She reached out and took him in her hands, caressing him as he grew larger and harder. Then he spread her legs and mounted her. When she felt the passion and strength of him inside her, Susa felt tears spring to her eyes. Kent had always felt right in her life, like a piece of puzzle that had somehow gotten lost but was now exactly where it needed to be.

Kent felt as if he was in a dream. A good one. The truth was he'd had this dream many times before. And now the torrent of emotion that came forth excited and soothed him somehow. He pulled her to him, exploring deeper and deeper inside of her. He felt her body tense and then give everything of herself over to him, her breath shallow, as he continued slow and deliberate until he felt her reach another crescent. Finally, when he couldn't hold back anymore, he came, crying out her name.

Susa slid from under him, and when Kent caught his breath, he turned sideways on the ripple of sheets to face her. She gazed at him, a look he couldn't define on her face.

"I see things going through you mind."

Susa nodded.

"What is it?" Kent asked, wanting to read her mind.

Susa's eyes searched his face.

"I wasn't kidding when I said I'd dreamed about this many times."

Susa got a puzzled look on her face. "You meant that?"

Kent moved closer, until they were inches apart. "Yes. You don't believe me?"

"I just thought…"

"What?"

"I just figured you've probably had so many girlfriends over the years. I mean. Oh, I don't know what I mean."

Kent reached and pulled her hard against him, his lips against Susa's when a phone buzzed.

They pulled apart.

"I'm afraid not to answer." Susa climbed out of bed and went across the room to get her phone. "Hermann, where are you?"

At the look of horror on her face, Kent bound out of bed to her. She pressed the speaker phone button.

"Bring us the diamonds, he won't lose any more fingers," said a man as someone cried out in pain in the background.

"Stop hurting him, please." Susa begged and began to sob. "Where do you want me to bring them?"

"I'll call back tomorrow with instructions. You bring the police into this, he dies." The line went dead.

By now, tears streamed down Susa's cheeks.

"Hermann is going to be fine. I promise you," Kent said, wrapping his arms around a sobbing Susa. "We'll talk to Joey and figure this thing out."

"He said no police."

"They always say that. We can trust Joey. Everything is going to be okay."

"What about his fingers?" She shivered. Her large eyes were filled with pain.

"They were probably bluffing, to get you to comply."

She nodded, lifting her chin and taking on a resolute look.

He took out his phone and dialed Joey's number. "It's me," said Kent. "You hear from Hermann?"

Kent explained the call they just got.

"Dammit. I've checked with all my sources. Nothing. I was going to visit that German gemologist tomorrow, but I have to be in court in the morning, and it could take all day."

"How about me and Susa go?"

"I don't know about that."

"Look, we're running against time here."

Joey sighed, then gave Kent the gemologist's address with some pointers on getting information out of the man.

When Kent told Susa they'd be going to see the jeweler first thing in the morning, she paced about the bedroom. "I don't know if I can sleep."

"How about we go outside and look through the telescope?"

"Looking at the moon will remind me of Hermann," Susa said. "I guess it doesn't matter, because I can't stop thinking about him."

Kent hugged his arm around her shoulder. "Maybe we'll see Uranus or Mars, or Pisces or Aries." He gave her his robe and put on a sweatshirt and his pajama bottoms. Snuggling into his robe helped calm Susa.

They went out onto the deck, and Kent set up the telescope. When Susa took a look, she saw a brilliant wash of twinkling stars, and several bright planets. "Wow, this is beautiful," she said, marveling at how clear everything looked. "I can see so much more in the sky with the telescope."

"You like microscopes, and telescopes are my thing," said Kent. "Look at the moon."

Susa directed the telescope to the moon and peered through the lens. "It really does look like Swiss cheese. Hermann used to swear that was the case, but I didn't believe him. Until now." Worry flooded her chest and she sighed.

"Just a minute." Kent went back inside and came out with two chairs and a large, heavy blanket. He motioned for Susa to sit down, then sat next to her and wrapped them both in the blanket. "A little moon gazing will help you relax," he murmured.

Susa rested her head against him and gazed at the sky. Before long, the tension in her body started to ebb, and she found herself dozing off on Kent's strong shoulder.

17

Kent woke early the next morning and smiled at the sound of Susa's soft snore and the sweet way her lashes feathered against her cheeks. He studied her pretty face. When she had fallen asleep next to him last night on the deck, he had picked her up and carried her to his bed. Her altercation at the park and worry about Hermann had clearly stressed her, and it was awhile before she truly settled. For the first couple of hours, she tossed and cried out Hermann's name.

Kent understood the bond. Growing up, it was him and Gloria against the world. If someone had his sister hostage, he'd be a wreck.

Susa's eyes sprang open, and Kent felt a ping in his heart when he saw a look of undisguised pleasure in them.

"Hi, sleepyhead," he said.

"Good morning," Susa said and sat up, pulling the sheet over her breasts. "Anything from Joey?"

Kent reached behind him for his phone on the nightstand. "No. Nothing."

He motioned to slide out of bed. "How about I make us some caffeinated beverages, and I've got some muffins, if you're hungry. The sooner we get on the road to the jewelers, the better."

Susa reached out and put her hand on his arm. "Thank you."

Kent took her hand and kissed it gently. "I'm here for you. You're not alone in this."

A half hour later, Kent was driving them through holiday traffic to the LA Jewelry District. As he raced in and out of lanes, he laughed when he saw Susa grip the side of her seat. "I take it my car is faster than yours?"

"I think it's the driving," she said.

"We'll be fine. I've been in hairier situations than this on the racetrack."

"Where did you race?" she asked, not letting go of her seat.

"I raced stock cars. Mostly in the south. I was sponsored and enjoyed it at first."

"At first?"

"It might not seem like it, but it's hard on the body, and mind. But the biggest reason was the fraud. I got approached by a group on the circuit that was having races thrown to game the system. I wouldn't play."

"That probably didn't go over well."

"Went over pretty bad. So bad that I think they rigged my car. That's how I got in the accident."

"Oh, Kent. I'm so sorry. Were they prosecuted?"

He checked his rearview mirror and made his way around a minivan. "I was going to report it. My sister kept bugging me about it, but it would have been hard to prove. She couldn't believe that I would give up that easily, but I was just tired of fighting. I got a settlement from the insurance company, so I decided to make a clean break and go to culinary school."

"I can understand that."

Kent glanced at Susa. "You can? Most people say I was an idiot."

"Sometimes there's more important things to do than fight. If you had, you might not be as fulfilled as you are and making all the delicious food you're making now."

Kent smiled. "And it sounds to me like you're making some important discoveries with your research?"

Susa brightened. "I hope so. The research does have the potential to help a lot of people. But I've been keeping kind of quiet about it. First, because I want to make sure it works. Plus, I don't necessarily trust my colleagues not to steal my work."

"No honor among scientists, huh?"

"Unfortunately, not always."

Kent pulled off the freeway and headed down 6th Street. Skyscrapers lined the way, jutting into the bright blue, cloudless December sky. He stopped the car in front of a crosswalk as a woman pushed a baby stroller past. When they reached a building that said International Jewelry Center, Kent drove down a side street and was surprised to find a parking space. He parallel parked, sandwiching his car between a Mercedes and a Toyota.

"How about we pretend to shop for a diamond ring for you?"

Susa looked surprised and laughed as she got out of the car. "I hope you brought your credit card."

They made their way to a jeweler on the corner. The door chimed as Kent pushed it open and motioned for Susa to enter. An older portly man looked up from a display case. "How may I help you?" he said, his German accent unmistakable.

Kent spoke up. "We're looking for a diamond ring for my lady."

The man's round face lit up. "That's marvelous. Come sit down. I'll show you some lovely pieces."

As Susa and Kent made themselves comfortable on plush gold chairs in front of the jewelry case, the man asked, "When is the big day?"

Susa spoke up. "August."

"Marvelous. Indoor or outdoor wedding?"

"Outdoors, in the evening, under the moonlight," said Kent, who saw out of the corner of his eye Susa staring at him.

"First things first," said the man, reaching out his hand. "My name is Hans. I will be happy to assist you in finding the perfect wedding ring."

"Thank you. I'm Kent, and this is my fiancé, Susa."

Hans gently took Susa's hand in his. "It looks like you are a size 7.

Would you like a solitaire and plain band? Or perhaps solitaire with a diamond band?" he asked her.

Susa scanned the display case. "I think a solitaire with a plain band."

"Wonderful. Are we looking for a carat or more?" Hans eyed the contents of the case, waiting for her answer.

Susa stole a glance at Kent, then asked, "Do you have any purple diamonds?"

The man looked up, eyes widening briefly. "You must have a substantial budget?" he asked Kent.

"Money's no object." Kent reached over and squeezed Susa's hand.

"At the moment, I don't have any purple diamonds. You may know that many come from the Argyle mine in Australia. That mine is now closed."

"I did know that," said Susa. "In fact, we heard you were the person to come to for purple diamonds."

The man straightened on his stool. "May I ask where you got your information?"

"A friend," said Kent, keeping his eyes trained on the man. "He said it wasn't common knowledge you had them."

The man crossed his arms on his chest. "What do you really want?" His tone had changed.

Kent leaned forward slightly. "We're looking for someone who used to work in the underground trade."

"And who might this person be?"

Kent decided to go with full transparency. "His name is Hermann St. James."

The man blinked. "How do you know Hermann?"

"He's my cousin," said Susa. "We're just trying to find him."

The man uncrossed his arms and placed his hands on the glass case. "I don't know where your cousin is, but I can tell you these are some very dangerous people he's involved with." He stood. "Now if you'll excuse me. I have much to do to prepare for last minute holiday shoppers."

Susa and Kent stood and left the store. When they walked out onto the street, he pulled her to him. "We'll find Hermann."

Susa stiffened then, her attention across the street. Kent glanced over to see several people walking. "What is it?" he asked.

"I thought I just saw Brad, Hermann's boyfriend, but now I can't tell. There's so many people."

"Why don't you call him? Say we want to stop by to update him," Kent suggested.

Susa pulled out her phone and found his name in her contacts and hit call.

"It's me, Susa. No word from Hermann?" Kent watched as she waited for a moment. "We've dug up a few things," she continued. "Can we stop by to update you?" Susa's eyebrows raised. "Okay, I understand." She ended the call. "That's odd. He says he was up all night worried and needs to take a nap now. He asked that we check in with him later."

18

"How about if we swing by your cousin's place and see if Brad's car is there?"

Susa agreed. But as soon as they got on the freeway, traffic was at a standstill.

Kent began drumming his thumbs on the steering wheel. "I'd say I could get in the fast lane, but even that's stopped. Nothing worse than holiday traffic. And I've never been a big fan of the holidays."

"Really? I would have thought it would be great to live somewhere with white Christmases."

"That part could be fun. It was the other stuff."

"What other stuff?"

Kent leaned forward in his seat and put a hand on his lower back and winced. "I broke a couple of vertebrae during the crash. My lower back tends to act up, especially when I've been driving for awhile."

"Want me to massage it?" asked Susa, leaning toward him.

"Sure. We're not going anywhere."

She reached behind his back and began kneading it. "It does seem tight."

"It's always tight, although PT has been helping. I missed my appointment today."

Susa stopped rubbing. "I'm sorry this whole thing is disrupting your life."

"I'm not. I haven't had this much excitement in a long time."

That made Susa happy. "You haven't? I would have thought you enjoy creating in the kitchen." The cars began moving in front of them, and she removed her hand as he started to drive.

"I love being a chef, especially on those nights when we're busy, but other than that I've been kind of bored."

"I guess I can understand that, after race car driving."

"That's not what I'm talking about."

"What are you talking about?"

Just then a car tried to sandwich itself in between them and the car in front of them.

"Dammit! What is that idiot doing?"

Was it Susa's imagination, or was Kent evading her questions?

Kent knew the questions about his childhood were inevitable now that he and Susa were getting closer. While he wanted to be honest, he didn't particularly want to discuss his past. When he was a kid, he often wished that he had the perfect family like he'd see on television, but he and Gloria's life was far from normal.

"Excuse me, miss, but there have been reports of a minor staying with you. Several of the neighbors have filed a complaint that he slashed their tires. Is he here?"

"I'm sorry, officer, but they must be mistaken. There's no minor staying with me."

From his hiding place in the hallway of the apartment, Kent could see the police officer scanning the living room.

"You're all alone here?"

"Yes, I am. And excuse me, but I'm going to be late for work."

The officer took one last look around. "Okay, you have a good night, miss."

When Gloria closed the door, Kent stayed where he was sitting on the floor against the wall across from the bedroom they shared. His sister came to tower above him. When he started to apologize, she stopped him.

"Did you slash their tires?"

Kent stood up. "No, it was that jerk Ricardo. I won't hang out with him anymore. I promise."

"Too late. We're on their radar now. What are you going to do? Stop going to school and stay inside all the time?"

Kent didn't say anything.

"Start packing while I'm at work tonight." Gloria sighed. "It's payday, so we can make a clean break. I'm thinking Louisiana."

"My story is boring," Kent said as the traffic started to pick up, and he made his way around a large truck. "Let's talk about you. Your mom and dad still alive?"

"Yes, they live in Anaheim and take my nephew to Disneyland constantly."

"That sounds like fun." Kent smiled. "What's your nephew's name?"

"Devan." Susa studied Kent's profile. Why did he refuse to talk about his past?

Kent glanced her way. "You okay?"

Susa flashed back to their intimate time together, then considered her words carefully before speaking. "I'm just wondering why you're being so evasive about your past."

Kent stared straight ahead as he drove, a frown on his face. Susa waited, holding her breath, hoping she hadn't made a mistake asking the question. Finally, he spoke. "My childhood was complicated. My sister and I had to run from town to town so that I wouldn't get picked up by Social Services. Most of the burden went to her. There was a lot of deception. Things I prefer not to think about."

"I didn't mean to pry," said Susa.

Kent looked at her, then back to the road. "We made our way okay. She's married to a great guy now."

Susa decided to gently keep going. "And your parents?"

"I don't remember my parents very well. They were older when they had me. They both died in a fire at our cabin in the Ozarks. Gloria got me out, but she couldn't save them. It hit her harder than me."

"Oh, that's terrible. How old were you when that happened?"

"I was eight, and Gloria was seventeen. It was Christmastime."

"So, that's why you don't like Christmas," said Susa. She leaned over and kissed Kent on the cheek softly, her heart happier when she saw the tense expression on his face soften. "No more talk about that, if you don't want," she said. "But thank you for telling me."

They drove the rest of the way to Orange County in silence. When they got off the freeway in Tustin, Susa directed Kent to Hermann's address. Soon, they came to her cousin's house. "Right here," she said. A sleigh filled with Christmas packages decorated the front lawn. White icicles hung from the eaves, and there was a big red bow tied around the mailbox. She let out a sigh of relief to see Brad's car in the driveway. "I guess I must have been mistaken. That's Brad's car."

Kent drove past and stopped a few houses down. "Either that or he beat us here. I'll be right back."

Kent got out of the car and walked back toward Hermann's house. She watched in the rearview mirror as he quickly went to the front of Brad's car and touched the hood. Then in long strides, he hurried back to the car, sliding in and shutting the door. "The hood was hot. That car just pulled into the driveway."

19

"For all we know," said Kent, "Brad is cheating on Hermann with someone in LA. Or maybe he was trying to get information and didn't want to worry you."

"This is all such a mess!" Susa sighed. "How could Hermann get involved with this sort of thing again?"

Kent reached out and squeezed her shoulder. "How about we stop at the restaurant for a little while and have something to eat? I need to check in."

When they arrived at the Tipping Whale a few minutes later, the early dinner rush had started. Kent led Susa to the kitchen, where they found a harried Ernesto shouting orders to Juana.

"Boss, glad you're here. Raul is out sick. We could use all hands on deck."

Kent looked at Susa.

"I can help, too," she said, pushing up her sleeves. "Just put me to work."

"You sure about that?" Kent asked.

"Of course. Where do I start?"

"Wash up, and I'll have you dice some vegetables," said Ernesto.

While Susa washed her hands, Ernesto gave Kent a sideways glance. "Looks like you worked things out after your flub up."

Kent smiled. "Yes."

"*Bueno.*" Ernesto laughed, giving Kent a quick jab in the arm.

"What's good?" asked Susa, drying her hands on a paper towel.

"That you're going to help." Ernesto grabbed an apron off a hook and handed it to her, pointing to a mound of vegetables on the butcher block counter. "How good are you with knives?"

"I'm a scientist. I dissect things."

Kent watched as Ernesto showed her how to dice up the vegetables. Before long she was cutting produce like a pro.

The next few hours went by in a whir like they always did on a busy night. The three of them took turns eating during the rush, and when the final meal was served, Kent and Susa sat down on stools, exhausted.

"I can't believe you and Ernesto cooked and served all those vegetables." They were alone in the kitchen while the others were out in the dining room.

"I bet your feet are tired."

Susa reached down to rub a foot. "It was fun, though. I can see why you like it. Quite an adrenaline rush trying to get everyone fed."

"Exactly."

Susa frowned.

"What?"

"I just realized I didn't think of Hermann the whole night." She got up and went to get her phone out of the cupboard where they stored personal items. "Oh, my god! An unknown number called several times."

"They'll call back," said Kent. Sure enough, the phone buzzed again. Susa answered and pushed speakerphone.

"Hermann, where are you?"

"I'm okay, but you need to give them the diamonds."

"Tell me where you are."

Kent heard muffled voices in the background, then Hermann returned to the phone. "They say you'll get a location tomorrow. Please, Susa, bring the gems."

"Hello! Hermann! Hello!" Susa shouted at the phone, tears in her eyes.

"He's gone," said Kent quietly.

Susa dug around in her purse and pulled out a tissue, then wiped her eyes. "I don't know how much more of this I can take."

Ernesto had come back into the kitchen and soon placed a cup of tea in her hands. "*Te de manzanilla.* My grandma always said it calmed her nerves."

"Chamomile. Thank you, Ernesto."

"I'm going to call Joey again," said Kent. "You okay?"

Susa nodded as she took a sip of tea.

Joey answered immediately. "I was just about to call you. We finally got our friend Willie from the rest stop to do some talking. I know who sent him, or at least who he says sent him."

"Who?"

"It's a big-time philanthropist. Simon Hewes. We're trying to figure out the connection. Willie is swearing up and down that he was hired by Hewes to get the diamonds. And he's begging for protection."

Kent told him about Hermann's call.

"Let me know as soon as you have that location. And tell Susa the fact that Hermann is still alive is a big thing. That doesn't always happen."

After he hung up, Kent asked Susa, "Do you know a Simon Hewes?"

Susa's brow furrowed. "That name sounds familiar."

"He's a local philanthropist. Would Hermann have had dealings with him? Willie is claiming Hewes sent him."

"Maybe he was a customer at the coffee shop?"

"Joey also wanted you to know it's a good sign Hermann is still alive."

Susa picked up the teabag and dunked it back into the cup. "I was just thinking about how whenever the going gets rough, Hermann always makes me laugh and see the bright side. I guess the fact that he's alive is the bright side." Susa met Kent's eyes, and he wished more than anything he could put a smile on her face.

"Remember that really hot day when he talked us into trying to fry eggs on the sidewalk?" Kent asked.

Susa laughed. "It actually works in Arizona where he grew up, but I told him it wasn't going to work in Georgia. All we did was make a terrible mess, and then his mother was mad we wasted eggs." She finished the rest of her tea.

"It's been a long night," said Kent. "Let's go back to my place and get some rest."

When Kent pulled into his driveway a while later, he said, "Will your car be okay at the lab?"

"It should be. There are employees coming and going all night." Susa sat up in her seat. "The lab has surveillance cameras outside. Joey could get those tapes, and we could see if Hermann was with someone the night he dropped off the diamonds."

"Great idea." Kent pulled his phone out of his pocket and texted Joey. Within seconds of sending the text, his phone rang. His screen said Gloria. "It's my sister."

"I'll wait outside the car," she whispered as Kent took the call.

"Is everything okay?" asked Gloria. "I haven't heard a word from you."

"Sort of. It's complicated."

"Tell me."

"Remember the girl I met at Lake Blue Ridge in Georgia that summer you were working at the lodge?"

"The pretty redhead? I swear her cousin was gay."

"That's them. Long story short, I met up with her a couple of nights ago. It turns out she's a scientist at UCI and works right down the street from the restaurant."

"I remember the way you two looked at each other," said Gloria.

"I was pretty crazy about her. Looks like I still am."

"Tell me more."

Kent laughed. "I'm working on the more right now. Actually, I have a question. Have you ever heard of Simon Hewes?"

"Who hasn't. He's one of Orange County's biggest philanthropists. Why?"

"He might have something to do with some kind of scheme a cop friend of mine is checking out. Know anything about him?"

"Well, remember the woman with the mansion in Newport I told you about? I've done some photography for her. A couple of weeks ago when I was getting ready to do a photo shoot of her dogs, of all things, I overheard her talking to a girlfriend about Hewes. The girlfriend's husband is good friends with him. Apparently, he's having a torrid affair with some high society woman living in the South somewhere."

"Thanks. That could be important."

"Count on me for crazy rich and famous stories. Hey, you sound happy."

Kent glanced outside to see Susa staring up at the stars. "I am."

"Is it the redhead? I saw that even back then. You were different after we left the lake. Sad. That's when you really started acting up and giving me gray hairs."

Kent felt a lump forming in his throat. "I'm sorry for everything I put you through."

"I still wouldn't trade it. You know that. And you turned out good. Just tell me you're not getting involved in something dangerous with that cop friend of yours. Let him handle his own whodunit."

"Don't worry about me."

When Kent hung up and got out of the car, he put his arm around Susa. "You didn't have to stand out here in the cold."

"I wanted to give you some privacy. All good with your sister?"

"She told me something very interesting about Hewes. He's having a heated affair with a wealthy woman who lives in the South."

"Maybe the diamonds are for her."

"Men have been known to do crazy things for love." Kent looked up at the moon suspended in the dark night sky.

20

When they got into the house, Kent checked the thermostat. "It looks like the heater is on the fritz again."

"Again?"

"I need to get it replaced. I'm used to colder winters, but you're a California girl."

"I guess you'll have to keep me warm." Susa smiled.

"I think it's my duty." Kent pulled her to him and gave her a long, slow kiss. When they came up for air, he said, "Let's hop in the hot tub on the deck."

"In this weather?"

"Haven't you ever been in a hot tub under the stars? Besides, you owe me. You chickened out the night we talked about skinny-dipping in the lake in Georgia."

Susa laughed. "Maybe I do."

"I keep the tub on the warm side during winter, but I'll go out and turn it up."

Susa waited as Kent went outside, her heart racing with excitement, eager to slip into the warm water and gaze up at the stars with him. Then her thoughts moved to Hermann, and she felt guilty being this happy.

Kent came back in, bringing with him a cold draft from outside. "The water is pretty warm already. But it'll get warmer in a little while. I'd suggest stripping here, then making a run for it. If you need some help, I'll be glad to assist." He grinned.

"Any crazy people out there with telescopes?" Susa giggled.

"Only me."

"I vote for taking our clothes off outside and jumping right in."

The hot tub was bubbling and sending swirls of vapor into the night. Susa quickly peeled off her clothes, squealing when the cold air hit her skin. She scampered up the steps leading to the tub, then slid into the deliciously warm water. Watching as Kent climbed in, she felt spellbound with delight at the sight of his long, muscled body silhouetted by the moonlit sky.

He came to crouch in front of where she sat, just his head exposed to the chilly night air.

"How does it feel?" he asked, over the sound of the tub's jets.

"Fabulous." Susa leaned back and sighed as jets massaged her back.

Kent looked up at the sky, then met her eyes with his. "Did you notice the moon was full the night we first met in Georgia, and it was full the other night when we found each other again?"

Susa felt her heart do a happy dance. "I did. You were walking out of the bowling alley that night. I remember you had a pale blue shirt on that reflected the moonlight."

Kent moved in closer, reaching out and guiding Susa's legs to wrap around him. With their faces nearly touching, he breathed, "How much do you remember about that summer?"

"All of it."

"I've never stopped thinking about you. All these years," Kent said as the water churned around them. He rubbed his fingertip across her lips, his expression becoming serious. "We were meant to be." He kissed her then, a long passionate kiss that sent Susa's senses into overdrive. She felt him grow hard against her as she straddled him.

"Make love to me," she whispered in his ear, kissing him and kissing him again. She felt his erection hard as it moved against her, arousing every one of her senses. His warm tongue searched her mouth as his hands caressed her back. Then he moved to sit on the ledge against the hot tub wall, pulling her to him. As he guided himself into her, Susa gasped and waited, the tension and desire filling every part of her body. Then she moved with him in the warm water, looking up at the starry sky above them. When he thrust himself in slowly over and over, kissing her neck, Susa buried her head against his wet skin. Then he held her by her bottom and pressed hard against her, until his body shuddered with the ecstasy Susa felt. She wanted to weep for the nights all those years she often dreamed of him. Instead, she took his face in her hands, studied every line, the deep blue eyes so earnest and loving. Then her heart thanked the stars overhead and the night she found him waiting for her.

When they finished catching their breaths and were huddled side-by-side on the ledge, Susa glanced up at the starry moon. "Do you remember the ceremonies Hermann had us do under the oak tree that summer?"

"What I remember the most is looking at you in the moonlight."

Susa laughed. "I was so distracted by you, I barely knew what I was doing. Hermann was fixated with gems and diamonds even then." She reached for Kent's hand in the bubbling water. "That last night you never showed up..." Susa had made a statement, but she knew it was really a question.

"I'm sorry I didn't have a chance to say goodbye," said Kent. "You and Hermann were the first real friends I ever had. But my sister and I had to leave suddenly. It was too painful to explain to you why, so I just disappeared." Kent continued, "I really started raising hell after that summer. It was tough on her."

Susa was silent as she considered what Kent just shared. The look on his face told Susa the details still pained him, so she decided not to press him about it.

"I want you to know everything, Susa." Kent was quiet for a moment. "I put some towels next to the deck when you're ready to jump out. We can dry off and make a beeline for bed."

Susa looked up at the night sky. "A few more minutes. It's so beautiful out here." What she really wanted was to memorize every moment of their night together. Every kiss, every feel of his body as he made love to her. Would she tell him she had agonized over losing him since they were young, and that she couldn't ever have loved a man the way she loved him? "Let's go to bed," she whispered.

He took her hand.

21

The next morning in bed, Susa turned to face Kent, putting her hands under her head. "I'm still in shock about us meeting up after all these years."

"And don't you think it's odd that we met twenty years later, just like Hermann said we would?" Kent asked. "Though not in Georgia."

Susa's brow furrowed at the thought of Hermann. "I'm beginning to wish I hadn't given the diamonds to Joey."

Kent raised his eyebrows. "Instead of trading them for Hermann?"

"There doesn't seem to be any other option. Could we at least get some back from Joey?"

"I doubt it." Kent turned to stare at the ceiling. "Maybe we could set something up and use me as bait."

"You. They've been calling me."

"No way I'm letting you go in as bait."

Now it was Susa's turn to raise eyebrows. "Really? I did pretty good at the rest stop."

Kent sighed. "You did, but I don't want you to be in that kind of danger again."

"What's the solution?"

"Let's go talk to Joey. Maybe we can figure something out together."

. . .

"Absolutely not." Joey leaned back in his office chair and pushed a lock of black hair off his forehead.

"They're supposed to call back today," said Susa. "They'll probably want to trade Hermann for the diamonds."

"I'm trying to find an undercover officer to go in your place."

"He's my cousin." Susa tried to quell her desperation, but it bubbled over. "I gave you the diamonds, and he's in a lot of danger. We need to do something now."

"Let me see if we can safely bring you into this. But we're not taking those gems out of the station. We'll have to use decoys." Joey leaned forward on his desk. "If we do need to send you in, Susa, which I'm hoping we don't, the trick will be to convince them that you're alone, that you have the diamonds, and that you're open to an even trade. Of course, we would be there to back you up. But let me think more on this first."

As they walked out into the chilly late morning air, Kent suggested, "How about we go to the restaurant while we wait? I have to prep for today's lunch. Or did you need to go to the lab?"

A car drove by with holiday music blasting. "I keep forgetting that it's almost Christmas," Susa said. "My car is at the lab. How about you drop me off. I'll go check in, then meet you at the restaurant."

Kent hesitated.

"I'll be careful," Susa assured him.

When Susa got into the lab, Bernard approached her immediately. "I noticed your car here early this morning, but you weren't around. Everything okay?"

Susa headed to her work area, Bernard at her heels. "Everything is fine. I was out getting samples."

"Anything interesting?" Bernard's question set Susa's nerves on edge. She needed to think, and he was making it difficult.

"Just working on my analyses. How about you? Did that assay pan out?"

"It's going really well. Thanks for your tips about that. I should have enough to finish my paper for the journal soon."

"That's great." Susa sat down at her laboratory table eager to look at the jimsonweed under the microscope.

When Kent arrived at the restaurant, the place was packed. He made his way into the kitchen to find a harried Ernesto barking orders at Raul, who was trying to prep a salad.

"*Hijole!* There you are," Ernesto said.

"You should have texted me. I didn't expect lunch to start early today." Kent looped his apron over his head and tied the ties.

"I didn't have time. Looks like the Christmas lunch rushes are starting earlier this year."

What Susa saw through the microscope looked promising, so she took the samples to the spectrometer. If the results coincided with the test she did on the brassica family of plants last week, she'd be well on her way to proving her hypothesis.

Studying the readout as she walked back to her work area, Susa's heart rate sped up. This had all been wildly hypothetical when she had started three years ago, but now it looked like her hunches had been right. The ramifications were so exciting, she wished she had someone to share it with. Then she remembered Kent waiting for her. She pulled her phone out of her pocket. No texts from him, but there had been a missed call from an unknown number twenty minutes earlier. She sat down on the stool, her breath catching in her throat. That must have been about Hermann. She had gotten too caught up in her work while her cousin's life hung in the balance.

Susa put her test results in her drawer, then sat there staring at the phone, willing it to ring. Certainly, they'd call back. Suddenly, the phone vibrated in her hand.

"Hello?"

"Your cousin has worn out his welcome. Bring the diamonds in the next thirty minutes, or he's dead." Susa held her breath as the voice on the phone gave her an address, then hung up before she could reply. She jotted the address down and quickly dialed Kent's number, but it went to voicemail. No answer from Joey either. Frantic that the caller meant what he said, she decided she had no other choice than to go herself. Grabbing a specimen bag from her workspace, she glanced around the lab. One of the researchers had left some shells out on the community workspace. Running over, she grabbed a handful and tossed them into the bag, then ran for the door.

"Susa?" Bernard said as she sped by, but she ignored him.

The lab door closed behind her, and she rushed toward the elevator. She had no idea what she was walking into. She just knew she couldn't wait around for Hermann to get murdered.

22

When Susa arrived at the address the man had given her, a tailor shop in Santa Ana, she pulled on the door, but it was locked. Taking a deep breath, she rapped several times. A hulk of a man with bulging biceps appeared. He yanked her inside, shutting the door behind her.

Rattled, Susa looked around the dimly lit shop, which smelled of cigarette smoke. She willed herself to stop shaking. "Where's Hermann?"

"Where's the diamonds?" The man had a southern accent.

She stared at him defiantly.

He responded by pulling a cellphone out of his pocket and dialing. "She's refusing to give me the stones." He listened for a moment, then handed her the phone. "Someone wants to talk to you."

"Hermann?"

"I assure you you'll be reunited once you hand over the diamonds," said a man's voice she didn't recognize.

"Hermann!" Susa called out, straining to listen through the line. Nothing.

"All will be revealed in good time," added the man, then he hung up.

The hulk grabbed her purse off her shoulder and emptied the contents onto a table containing bolts of fabric.

"They're not in there," Susa cried.

He picked up her phone and removed the SIM card, breaking the card in half and dropping it all back on the table.

Susa felt the blood rush to her ears, realizing how stupid she'd been to walk into this trap.

"Is Hermann even here?"

The man said nothing.

Just then she sensed a movement behind her, and a horrible-smelling cloth covered her mouth and nose before all went black.

When they'd finished with the lunch rush, Kent checked his phone. Susa had tried to call a few minutes ago. He quickly called back, but it went straight to voicemail. He waited five minutes and tried again. Still voicemail. Finding the UCI laboratory number online, he dialed it. An operator told him to hold while she paged Susa.

"I'm sorry, sir, Ms. York didn't answer. There is no record of her signing out, though, so she must still be in the building. Whom shall I tell her was calling?"

Kent gave her his name and hung up, taking deep breaths to offset the shallow ones. Maybe she was in the middle of something and too focused to hear the page. That sounded like Susa. But thirty minutes later, he still hadn't heard from her, so he called again.

The same operator answered. "Let me call the laboratory for you, sir." Kent waited, his anxiety level rising with each passing second. Finally, the operator came back on the line.

"According to a colleague, she rushed out of the lab about an hour ago without signing out. He has no idea where she went. He said she looked upset."

Kent hung up, cursing himself for leaving her alone. He called Joey, who answered after a couple of rings. "I noticed Susa called."

"She called you?" Kent asked.

"About an hour ago now. She's not with you?"

Alarm bells sounded in Kent's head as he told Joey what he knew.

"I'll check her last location before the phone powered off," Joey said. "What the hell happened?"

"Maybe she got a call about Hermann and went to meet with them."

"Without the diamonds."

"She's so afraid for her cousin. I shouldn't have let her out of my sight."

"I just got her last location," Joey said. "Looks like a tailor shop. 554 Lemon in Santa Ana. I'll meet you there."

When Kent arrived at the shop, he saw onlookers milling about, and an officer guarding the doorway. He rushed to the door. "I know Detective Landau," he said. The officer put out his hand to stop Kent from entering and turned his head to shout, "Detective Landau. There's someone here saying he knows you."

Joey came to the door, and Kent's knees threatened to buckle at the somber look on his face. "You can let him in," he told the officer, who stepped aside.

"There's no one here, but we did find Susa's purse, including her phone," said Joey. "And we just found a door to a hidden space in the back. It could be a saferoom, or…" Joey trailed off.

Horror filled Kent as he recalled Hermann's finger. "Did you get in?"

"It's got a heavy-duty locking system. Some techs are working on it right now."

Just then a CSI officer came and handed Joey a bag with the UCI logo marked specimens. With a gloved hand, Joey reached inside and pulled out a handful of shells.

Kent looked up at the ceiling. "Jesus, Susa."

Joey handed the bag back and told the officer, "Put this in evidence."

"Detective?" A technician yelled from the back of the shop.

"You stay here," Joey instructed Kent.

Kent tried to wait but worry propelled him to follow Joey. When he was several feet away from the door they had just opened, he heard Joey say, "Ah, Christ."

"Is it Susa?" Kent asked.

Joey turned around and put out a hand to stop Kent from coming any closer. "You don't want to see this."

"Hermann?" Kent asked.

"No, it's the guy Willie from the rest stop. Someone bailed him out today."

Joey put his hands on Kent's arms and held them firm. "The guy was shot through the head. Most likely because he didn't get the diamonds like he was supposed to. But, until they have the diamonds," he looked Kent in the eye, "Susa and Hermann will very likely stay alive."

23

Susa woke up groggy, her head pounding. She was lying on her back in a bed, staring at a bare bulb hanging from the ceiling. Motioning to sit up, her head began swirling and she lay back down. Once the bed stopped spinning, she strained to hear men's voices in the other room. Struggling through the fog in her head, she recalled the tailor shop and someone putting a rag on her face. Her nostrils flared at the memory of the stench of chloroform. Just then, footsteps headed toward the door. Susa closed her eyes, pretending to still be out.

Someone came to the side of the bed. "She should be up by now."

"Is she okay?" It was the man's voice from the tailor shop.

"Maybe I gave her a little too much."

"She better be okay. The boss wants her untouched."

"She'll be awake soon. How's our other guest?"

"Complaining, as usual."

The footsteps left the room, and Susa heard the door shut. She peeked out of half-opened eyes into the empty room, hoping to see Hermann.

Kent watched Joey assess the crime scene, feeling helpless.

"Is there something I can do?" he finally asked.

"Yeah, let me know the second you hear from Susa."

"How the hell am I going to hear from her if her phone is here?" Kent had watched as the CSI team bagged up Susa's belongings, including her cell.

"You never know. Answer any number that comes in." A crime scene investigator approached Joey then.

Kent waved Joey to continue and left the building. Out in his car, he leaned his forehead on the steering wheel. He thought about being with Susa in the hot tub last night. How right it felt. Life couldn't be that cruel, could it? To bring her back, then take her away like this? He reached over to his glove compartment and popped it open, taking out a bottle of ibuprofen. Opening it, he shook the maximum dose into his hand, then washed it down with the remnants of his morning coffee.

When Kent walked into the kitchen of the Tipping Whale, Ernesto frowned. "You look like hell."

Kent glanced down at a pile of shrimp Ernesto was deveining. "Scampi for tonight?"

"Yeah. You okay?"

Kent wiped his hand over his face. "Susa is missing. The police can't track her. Her phone was left at the scene."

Ernesto put down a shrimp and met Kent's gaze. "Scene?"

Juana came into the kitchen then and went to the back room where they kept supplies. Kent waited until she was out of earshot. "Yes, crime scene."

"Shit."

"And I don't know what to do."

"There's got to be someone who might know where she could be."

Why had Kent not thought about this before? There was someone. Kent was going to go right now and beat information out of him, if necessary.

Susa lay in the bed, her stomach clenching as waves of nausea threatened to make her wretch. She thought about the events of the last few days and struggled to put together the puzzle. Obviously, they wanted the diamonds. But she felt like there was a missing piece she just wasn't seeing.

The door opened before Susa could shut her eyes again. It was the man from the tailor shop. "So, you are awake," he said.

"I want to see Hermann."

"Very demanding for a little thing." He advanced toward her, his cowboy boots clacking on the floor. "Where are the diamonds?"

"I'm not telling you anything until you take me to my cousin."

"She's as stubborn as him, looks like," said a tall man, who appeared in the doorway. "Should we convince her to talk?"

Susa's heart sped up at his words.

"No, take her to him. She can watch while we chop off a few digits."

The tall man came across the room in quick strides, grabbing Susa by one arm and yanking her off the bed. "No tricky business, or your cousin will pay the price." He guided her through a hallway and out into a sparsely furnished living room shrouded in late afternoon light. From there, he led her into a kitchen, then out the back door. On the ground, next to the house was a basement door. The man from the tailor shop lifted the door, exposing a gun under his jacket as he did so.

"Walk downstairs slowly," instructed the man holding her. He let go, and they both followed behind her.

When they were in the dark, dank space, the man from the tailor shop shined a flashlight on a padlocked door, then took out a key chain and unlocked it. As he did so, the tall man held Susa up against him. He smelled like whiskey and sweat, and she felt another wave of nausea and fear sweep through her.

Once the padlock was off, the man flipped on a light switch located on the outside wall, then swung the door open. Ever since they were kids, Hermann hated the dark, thought Susa as she was pushed through the threshold.

There, sitting on the floor against the far wall, sat Hermann, blinking in the light. At the look of relief mixed with terror in his eyes, she started sobbing.

24

Kent pounded on Brad's door so hard, it hurt his hand. "I know you're in there. Open the damn door!"

The door cracked slightly, and Brad peered out. "What the hell?"

Kent pushed the door open and entered the house. "We need to talk."

"Is this about Hermann?" Hope was written on Brad's face. "Have the police found him? I've been checking in with your officer friend."

Kent slammed the front door, and advanced toward Brad, who backed up into the living room. "I don't know why you're here," he said, "and you're making me uncomfortable."

"What were you doing in LA yesterday?"

Brad's eyes widened.

"Susa saw you. And now she's missing, too. The common denominator here is you."

"It's not what you think."

Kent pushed Brad back onto the sofa. "You're going to tell me exactly what's going on, and I better believe it."

"Okay, look, someone called me yesterday and said that if I didn't figure out where the diamonds were that they were going to begin to take off Hermann's fingers until there weren't any fingers left. I turned his things upside down and found this card. He reached into his back pocket and pulled out a white card with black lettering.

"Alfonso's Deli," read Kent. "Did you go there?"

Brad nodded. "Alfonso's cousin Gustavo is one of Hermann's old business partners, but he said he hasn't seen him for months."

"You believe him?"

Brad threw up his arms and slapped them down on the couch beside him. "I don't know. Two days ago, I thought Hermann was just a barista."

"Why did you lie to Susa about being in LA?"

"I didn't want to get her hopes up."

Kent eyed a number scrawled on the back of the card. "I take it this is Gustavo's number? Call him and see what he knows about Simon Hewes." He handed the card back to Brad.

Looking dubious, Brad tapped the number into his cellphone. "Hi, it's Brad. We met yesterday. Uh…" He looked up at Kent. "What do you know about Simon Hewes?"

Brad listened for a minute, then appeared to agree with Gustavo and hung up. "He said he couldn't talk about it on the phone. I'm supposed to meet up with him back in LA. He asked me to bring some cash."

Kent raised his eyebrows.

"He said he knows what Hewes wants," Brad added.

"I'll go meet him."

Brad didn't protest but gave him Gustavo's location. A few minutes later after visiting the ATM for cash, Kent was barreling down the freeway headed toward LA. It was just after seven, and rush hour traffic had started to ebb. Thirty minutes later, he pulled in front of a strip club on the outskirts of Hollywood. When he got out of the car, a muscle-bound guy covered in tattoos approached.

"Nice wheels, *amigo*, but that spot is reserved."

"I'm here to see Gustavo," said Kent.

"He's not expecting any visitors."

"Tell him I'm Brad's replacement."

The man lumbered into the club and returned shortly. "He'll see you.

But you need to pay for your parking spot before you leave, or we'll be taking your car."

Kent brushed past the man and entered the dimly lit club. A lone stripper slowly gyrated in front of a bald man in a red tank top hunched over at a nearby table. The man gestured to the girl, who leaned over to show him the full expanse of her breasts.

Kent walked over to the table. "Gustavo?"

"Where's Brad?" asked the man, checking out Kent from the corner of his eye.

"He's sitting this one out. I need some information. I'll pay well."

Gustavo took a slug of beer, and the foam clung to his mustache. He didn't respond.

"I need information on Simon Hewes," Kent continued, sitting down next to him.

Gustavo wiped his mustache with the back of his hand. "You come to a Mexican strip club to ask about some rich gringo?"

"I'm told you're the man to talk to."

A curvy waitress came up. "Want something, honey?"

"I'll have what he's having," said Kent.

She nodded and went to the bar.

"I want to make a deal with Hewes involving diamonds. Purple ones."

Gustavo whistled when a new girl with long, jet black hair came onto the stage. "And what does that have to do with me?"

"I know you've worked with Hermann in the past. This would help him out. If you've heard something valuable you can share, I'll pay. Five hundred.

The new stripper had come to undulate in front of Gustavo, who stuck a twenty-dollar bill into her G-string. He watched her slowly turn and walk to the center of the stage.

"How do I know you're not a cop?" Gustavo gave him a sidelong glance.

"You don't," said Kent as the waitress set a beer in front of him. He reached into his pocket and pulled out a wad of cash, tore off a twenty and handed it to her.

Gustavo glanced around the bar and then said in a low voice, "Hewes collects rare diamonds on the black market and resells them to the highest bidder. He's expecting a stash of purple diamonds tomorrow night. But word on the street is that the diamonds are missing."

"Where is the stash supposed to show up?"

Gustavo put out his hand to Kent, who responded by slapping the bills on the table. The man eyed the money, and then said, "Georgia."

"You two have five minutes for your family reunion. When I come back, I want to know where the diamonds are."

Susa ran to Hermann, taking his hands in hers. "All your fingers are still there, thank god." He had a swollen mouth and chin, and blood covered the front of his white shirt. "You have no idea how glad I am to see you."

"I'm not glad to see you," Hermann said, looking chagrined. "I was hoping you were somewhere safe." He grimaced as he shifted against the wall.

"What hurts?" asked Susa.

"My ribs, everything. It doesn't matter. Let's end this. Where are the diamonds?"

"There might be a problem with that."

Terror filled Hermann's face. "Susa, please tell me that someone didn't get them."

"Not exactly. The police have them."

"Why? Do you know what this means? These guys are going to slit our throats."

"I wasn't sure what to do. This guy attacked me in the street and told me to give the bag to him, and then Kent, Rogue, showed up and knows this detective named Joey, who's looking for you."

"Wait. What? Rogue? The guy from the lake in Georgia?"

"Can you believe it? He's a chef at a restaurant near the lab. His real name is Kent."

All the color drained from Hermann's face.

"It's a shock, I know."

"Susa. That summer. The ring you buried."

"That cubic zirconia? What does that have to do with this?"

"That wasn't a cubic zirconia, Susa. It was the real thing."

25

"Why on earth would you give me a real diamond ring to bury?"

"That summer, I was hanging out with this guy. Remember him?"

Susa rubbed the base of her neck, willing the pounding to stop. "I don't think so."

"Anyway, he hated his dad, so we got into his stash and took an old family heirloom. He told me to sell it, but I figured that would be bad karma. I had us bury it in that ceremony to bring us good luck. I figured we could always go back for it in twenty years, if no one claimed it. I know, the whole thing sounds totally insane."

Susa thought for a moment. "Did you tell them where the diamonds are?"

"No."

"We could say we have to go get them."

"Okay, but where would we lead them?"

The door swung open then, and in walked a well-dressed man in his late fifties. He had a determined look on his face.

"You're Simon Hewes," said Susa.

"And you're Susa York. The woman holding my diamonds. Where are they?"

"I'll tell you where they are when you let us go," she said.

The man got a contemplative look on his face. "And how does that work, exactly? I let you go, and then you, what? Send them to me in the mail?" He walked over and put one of his shiny black shoes on top of Hermann's hand and pressed as Hermann shouted, "Ow!"

"Stop!" Susa pleaded.

Slowly removing his shoe, he glared down at Susa, his eyes reflecting an unsettling glint. His phone buzzed, and he checked the screen. "I'll be back, and you're going to tell me where the diamonds are, or I will do much worse to your cousin's hand."

Kent left the strip bar more worried than when he'd arrived. He gave the guy watching his car some cash and got in and dialed Joey's number.

"Nothing yet," Joey answered. "Anything on your end?"

"I think so." Kent relayed Gustavo's lead about Georgia.

Joey sighed. "This all sounds a bit farfetched you know."

"Well, we all met in Georgia, and Hewes is said to have a mistress there. You still at the station? I can come down. Just don't tell me to go home and wait by the phone."

"Kent, please. I'm okay."

"You've got a black eye, Gloria. And I know it's not the first time he hit you." Kent held his fists so tight; he wasn't sure he could release them. "I'm done watching you get kicked around by that asshole." He started heading for the front door.

Gloria ran to the door and blocked it. "Just let this go. Next time the cops are going to catch you. Then they'll find out how old you are."

Kent felt his anger ebb at the pleading look in his sister's eyes. "You can't keep letting him do this to you, sis."

"I told him I was done. Okay? I even quit tonight."

"You did?"

"And I have no idea how we're going to pay the rent next week." Gloria wrapped her arms around herself.

"We've got the money I saved from the car shop."

"That is for you to go to college."

"No, Gloria. Right now, that money is for us to take care of ourselves. We're all we've got." Kent didn't have the heart to tell his sister that he didn't think he was college material.

When Kent pulled up in front of the Santa Ana Police Department, Joey stood outside. He walked over to the car.

"What's the matter?" said Kent.

"I just briefed my boss, and he's turning our case over to the FBI."

"What? We're going to have a bunch of strangers looking for Susa. This could get her killed."

"They've got jurisdiction. I'm not authorized to help you in Georgia. Plus, I just got put on a local robbery homicide."

"Well, I'm not sitting around on my hands. I know my way around Georgia."

"I wish there was more I could do," said Joey.

"Actually, there is something."

"Anything."

"I need one of the diamonds for a bargaining chip."

"Shit, Kent, anything but that."

"Does the FBI have them already?"

"Not yet, but you're asking me to put my job on the line."

"Susa's life is on the line. Just one." Kent held his breath while Joey considered.

Finally, Joey replied. "I'll tell the officer at the evidence locker that I need to take one last look at them."

"I'm sorry to put you in a tight spot," said Kent. "I'm desperate."

"I get it. I'd do anything for Iris. Wait here. I'll be back as soon as I can."

While Joey was gone, Kent made reservations for an early morning flight to Atlanta. He just prayed he'd be heading toward Susa, not away from her.

26

After Hewes left, he turned off the light, plunging the room into darkness.

"I'm so sorry, cuz. I should never have given you those diamonds," said Hermann.

"Where did they come from?"

"A girl in a hoodie when I was closing up the coffee shop one night last week. She laid them on me and ran away. I couldn't go to the cops. With my background, they would have thought I stole them. I was checking with my sources when I felt like someone was watching me, so I gave them to you. Before I knew it, someone nabbed me on the street and brought me here."

Just then, the door slammed open. Hewes stood in the doorway silhouetted by the bright light coming from the hallway. "Time's up." Two muscular men stood guard behind him.

"The diamonds are out of state," said Susa. "In Georgia." She caught Hermann's surprised face from the corner of her eye, but kept her gaze trained on Hewes. She noted a blink of shock on the man's face when she mentioned the location.

Hewes narrowed his eyes. "You better not be screwing around with me."

"They're at Lake Blue Ridge," Susa continued. She could see a vein on the side of Hewes's neck pulsing. The man turned on his heels and left the room, slamming the door and turning off the light again.

After Joey slid a small bag into Kent's hands outside of the police station and told him to be careful, Kent headed home. When he got in the house, he took the bag out of his pocket and shook the diamond into his hand, admiring it under the kitchen light. It was gorgeous with its purple tint. He put it back in his pocket and went to the bedroom to throw things into a bag, including a document that he took out of his desk drawer and signed. Then he took a piece of stationary out and began writing.

On his way out the door a few minutes later, Kent's eye fell on Susa's bonsai sitting on the table near the window. He remembered what she said about it needing a lot of care. He took it to the kitchen sink and splashed water on it. "Wish me luck," he said to the tree. Then he put it back and headed for the Tipping Whale. He needed to talk to Ernesto before going to the airport.

When he pulled into the restaurant's parking lot, he was glad to see Ernesto's car. That meant he was already in the kitchen prepping the dough for tomorrow's breads. He unlocked the front door to the sound of salsa tunes blaring from the back. When he pushed open the kitchen door, he found Ernesto pouring a bag of flour into the large mixer. He waved his arms to get his attention.

Seeing Kent, Ernesto let the bag slide down on the counter, creating a billow of particles, then went over to the sound system and turned off the music.

"Boss! Did you find Susa?"

"I know you've been taking up the slack here, and I really appreciate it," said Kent. "I've got to go out of town this morning. I think I know where Susa is. Can you continue to hold down the fort? Hire in some temporary help, if needed. And, can you sign these?" Kent placed some papers on the butcher block.

Ernesto wiped the flour from his hands and picked up the papers, his brow furrowing as he read them. "*Hijole*, boss, you're scaring me."

"Hopefully it doesn't come to this, but if something does happen to me, I want to know the restaurant is in good hands."

"I can't."

"You can," said Kent. He pulled a pen out of his pants pocket and handed it to Ernesto. "Please sign it. It'll set my mind at rest, and I need that right now."

Ernesto stared at him for a long while. "Boss, you sure about this?" When Kent didn't speak, Ernesto nodded and signed the papers.

Kent then handed him a letter with Gloria's name on it. "Please give this to my sister, if I don't come back."

"You've got my word," said Ernesto, who reached out to put a hand on Kent's shoulder. "*Que te vaya bien*," he said, wishing him good luck.

A few minutes later, two henchmen came and slid cloth bags on Susa's and Hermann's heads. From there, they were walked up and out of the basement and pushed into a car. Susa could feel both men flanking them as the car headed away.

Before long, the car stopped again, and Susa heard the telltale whine of a plane's engine. Susa's bag was yanked off her head. She looked out at a private airfield and a small jet.

"Those diamonds better be in Georgia," said Hewes.

As they were led to the plane, Susa shivered in the cold air, realizing she wasn't at all dressed for Georgia in December. But that was the least of her worries. She didn't want to think about what Hewes would do when he realized he was on a wild goose chase.

In the plane, Hewes had the men separate Susa and Hermann, then made himself comfortable, taking off his jacket and loosening his tie. He sat down across from Susa and picked up an *LA Times*. She looked beyond the front-page headlines, noting the pale light outside. It must be near dawn. For a moment, she allowed herself to think about Kent and how worried he must be. She wished she was at his house in the woods with him right now.

Susa put her head back against the soft pillowed chair of the airplane, her brain scrambling for a way out of this. When she'd gone through a dozen or more escape plans and rejected every one of them, she closed her eyes meaning to simply rest them but found herself dozing off.

When Susa awoke, the sun was bright outside the plane. Someone had set a tray of food in front of her. She looked over at Hermann to see him eating.

Hewes closed his laptop. "Eat your eggs. You need to keep your strength up. Much will be expected of you today, Ms. York."

Susa didn't answer as a lump of dread formed at the pit of her stomach. All she and Hermann had managed to do was delay the inevitable. Now they were almost in Georgia away from home and Kent and Brad. They'd soon be expected to produce the diamonds, and they couldn't. She knew they would become a liability at that point, and men like this didn't keep liabilities around for long.

27

When Kent pushed his carry-on into the overhead bin, he scanned the surrounding passengers to see if anyone appeared to be following him. An older woman across the aisle sat reading a book, a young mom rubbed the head of a sleepy child lying across her lap. Two teenagers sat next to each other checking their cellphones.

Kent's intuition had always been finely tuned. Probably from living the way he and Gloria had done all those years. He'd usually know when it was time to leave a place, because a neighbor had caught on that there were no parents in the picture.

He made himself comfortable in the window seat while a flight attendant's voice came over the intercom to announce that the pilot was preparing for takeoff. The flight would take four hours. Kent tightened his seat belt and took a deep breath. As far as he was concerned, five minutes was too long.

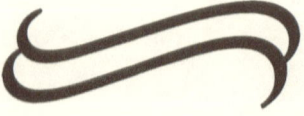

When the plane coasted to a stop, Susa glanced out the window to see that they'd landed on a small airfield. The sun shone bright, but she could tell it was cold outside from the surrounding bare trees and patches of snow on the ground.

Hewes stood and stretched, reaching down for the coat sitting beside him. After slipping it on, his phone buzzed and he checked it, then walked off the plane.

Susa went over to Hermann. "Did you get enough food?" She handed him a packet of cookies.

"Thanks hon," he said, his voice tight with anxiety as he put the package in his pocket. "Any bright ideas while we were flying?"

"Nothing that will work. You?"

Hermann shook his head.

"Hewes said, 'Things will be expected of me.' "

"That was ominous." Hermann agreed.

The chill coming in from the open door had started to permeate the plane. Susa rubbed her hands on her arms. "What's our plan?" She glanced out the window to see Hewes talking to a guard.

"How about we lead them to the old oak tree and do some digging and hope that the ring is still there," suggested Hermann. "Maybe it's not the diamonds he's looking for, but I understand it's worth a fortune."

Susa heard someone walking up into the plane and rushed back to her seat. Hewes stalked in and threw a coat at her and another at Hermann. "We've got a long drive to the lake."

The guard came back on the plane and grabbed Hermann, pulling him to his feet. He waited impatiently as Hermann put his coat on. Susa took the cue and stood up to put hers on. "Go straight to the car," said Hewes. "No trying to run. This airfield is surrounded by miles of forest. You won't get far before freezing to death."

The word death hung in the air as Susa and Hermann walked down the plane's stairs. Marching them over to a black SUV, the guard motioned for them to get inside. Then he shut the car door and waited outside next to it. The back windows were tinted, but Susa could see Hewes making another phone call.

Hermann sighed. "Brad must be so worried."

When Susa stiffened at his comment, Hermann noticed. "What?"

She shifted in her seat. "I told Brad about your past when we were at the police station. I'm sorry. I had to tell the detective." She wasn't about to tell him that Brad could be the reason they'd been kidnapped.

Hermann put his head in his hands. "It was bound to come out. To tell you the truth, it's kind of a relief." He looked over at Susa. "I'll be more relieved if we can come up with a plan for getting out of this mess. Does your aunt still have the lake house?"

"Yes. It's probably boarded up for the winter, though."

"We'll tell them to go there first. I've got an idea."

Just then Hewes opened the door and climbed into the passenger seat while his guard took the driver's side.

He turned to them, his breath forming vapor in the cold air. "Give me the address where the diamonds are."

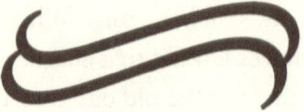

When the plane touched down in Atlanta, Kent got off as fast as possible and went straight to the rental car kiosks. Glancing behind him every few seconds, he ordered a sedan and grabbed the keys, then sprinted out the door toward the lot.

Ten minutes later, he put Lake Blue Ridge into the GPS and waited for direction. One hour and forty-seven minutes and he'd be at the lake, and hopefully close to Susa. He gunned the engine as he got on Interstate 75 heading north. It was tempting to push past the speed limit, but he couldn't afford to get stopped this time.

"Kent. Thank God." Gloria stood over the hospital bed as Kent tried to focus on her face. She squeezed his hand. "I thought I might lose you."

"What happened?" Kent gasped through the pain.

"You don't remember?"

Visions flashed in his mind. Being told to throw the race. Stomping off to his car. Revving the engine.

"Not really."

Concern filled his sister's eyes. "It's okay. All that matters is you're alive."

Kent's face hurt the most. He was going to ask Gloria about it, but darkness took over.

No one spoke as they made their way in the SUV to Aunt Marion's lake house. Susa tried to imagine what kind of idea Hermann might have. She also wondered if her aunt kept the spare key in the same place. It had been a few years since Susa had visited. In the silence, she couldn't help thinking about Kent, so far away from her now. Would she ever see him again?

At one point, Hewes got a phone call. Susa watched closely as he checked the screen, hesitated, then answered. "We're on our way now."

Hewes tensed while he listened to the caller. "I know. We'll clean up any loose ends."

When they pulled up in front of the cabin, it was late afternoon. The guard turned off the car, and Hewes checked out the building in the dimming light. He turned back to look at Susa and Hermann, his eyes flashing. "You better not be screwing with me."

"The diamonds are here," said Hermann.

"Get out and unlock the front door," he ordered Hermann. "Jorge, go with him. I'll stay with Ms. York."

Susa tried not to wince as she saw Hermann hobble to the front door. Running his fingers over the door rafter, he pulled off the key. Jorge took it from him and opened the screen door, inserting the key into the lock, and the two of them disappeared inside.

Before long, Jorge came out of the house and headed to the car. Hewes opened his window. "Do you have them?"

"There's a safe, but he says he needs her to open it." Jorge gestured with his head toward Susa.

"A safe. Sounds promising. Take her in."

Jorge pulled open Susa's door and reached for her arm, but she shrank away from him. "I can get out myself." She exited the car and walked toward the cabin, her mind pinging as she struggled to figure out what they were going to do when Hewes found out she couldn't open the safe.

They headed through the front room and toward the back of the cabin, where a light shone from her aunt's bedroom. Hermann's hands were bound to one poster of the bed and a wall safe had been exposed. A picture sat on the floor against the wall.

"Hopefully you remember the combination," said Hermann.

Susa went to the safe and dialed her aunt's birthday, Jorge right behind her. When it didn't open, she tried the same numbers again. Still no luck. "I'm sorry, those are the right numbers. She must have changed the combination."

Jorge took Susa by the shoulders and pushed her down on the other end of the bed. He tied her to the opposite bedpost, then stomped out of the room.

"That was your big idea?" Susa hissed.

"I'm trying to buy us time."

"For what? The inevitable?"

The front door opened and closed, and loud footsteps advanced toward the room.

Hewes came storming in. "If you have deceived me, losing your fingers will be the least of your worries." He directed his wrath at Hermann.

"There's diamonds in the safe," Herman insisted. "It just looks like the combination has been changed."

Hewes threw up his hands and left the room. When he returned, he announced, "Someone will be here soon with a blowtorch." He pointed to Susa. "Untie her, Jorge. She's coming with me."

Terror overtook Susa as Hewes suddenly brandished a gun.

28

Kent pulled off the highway at the Lake Blue Ridge sign and headed toward the water. As he drove slowly down the deserted streets, visions of that long-ago summer here at the lake flashed through his mind. The first time he'd seen Susa in front of the bowling alley that night. The bright smile across her face when their eyes met. When he neared a stand of trees next to the lake, he slowed to a crawl, searching the quickly dimming scenery. He spotted a giant tree several yards off the roadway and stopped the car, Hermann's words from two decades ago sounding in his ears.

"We shall meet here at this exact spot in the year 2019."

Kent got out of the car and turned on his cellphone flashlight, examining the frozen ground near the base of the old oak. His muscles clenched in the cold winter air. He'd been in such a hurry leaving California that he'd only brought a lightweight jacket. Crouching down, he felt the ground around the tree's trunk. He was pretty sure this was the spot.

He headed back to the rental car and popped the trunk, pulling out the tire iron from the spare kit. Back at the tree, he started digging.

As Hewes drove Susa along a forested road past cabins with smoke pluming from the chimneys, the day shortened, dusk now settling around them. He soon turned onto a long, gravel drive, the car bumping up and down as they went. At the end of the drive, they stopped in front of an industrial building. A dog barked when Hewes turned off the car. "Do as you're told, and you won't get hurt," he said, opening the driver's side door and pulling his gun from under the seat. He then opened her door and gestured to the building.

Susa got out of the car and, legs shaking, walked toward the front door, with Hewes right behind her. The door swung open, and an older man stood there. He looked vaguely familiar to Susa, but she couldn't place him.

"She's all yours," said Hewes, and left.

The man gave her an eerie smile as he closed the door. "Come in, Ms. York, or shall I call you Susa? I've heard quite a bit about you."

They stood in what appeared to be a waiting room.

"Please come with me," the man continued. As if reading her mind, he added, "I advise not trying to make a run for it. Electronic fencing surrounds the property."

He walked to a set of double doors and unlocked one. Pushing it open, he motioned for her to walk through. The moment she entered the room, the smell of formaldehyde hit her. She stood in an immense laboratory. There were tables in the center of the room and a wide variety of high-end scientific instruments along the walls. Momentarily forgetting she was being held against her will, Susa walked farther into the room, her pulse quickening. She'd never seen a lab this state-of-the-art in person. She admired a spectrometer that she knew cost more than five years of her salary.

"I'm told this is all the latest scientific gadgetry." The man beamed, looking around the room.

"This isn't your lab?"

"Oh, it is. But my son set it up. He designed the entire facility."

Just then a door at the back of the lab opened. Susa gasped. "Bernard, what are you doing here?" She struggled to put the pieces together as he advanced toward her, a smirk on his face.

"The great Susa York hasn't figured that out yet?" He wore a bright white lab coat with an apothecary insignia on the pocket. "Welcome to my lab," he announced.

"Your lab?"

"The only reason I've been working at that rinky-dink UCI lab was to get close to you and your research."

Susa stepped back at the unsettling look in Bernard's eyes. She felt her breath coming out in short gasps as she tried to rectify this Bernard with the one she knew in the lab. "Are you upset that I jilted you?"

Bernard threw back his head and laughed. "Jilted me? I'm gay, Susa. You're so obtuse, always with your head in your research." He advanced toward her, and Susa stepped back, bumping into the edge of a counter.

"You're the one Hermann was seeing all those years ago at the lake." Susa said. "You stole your father's diamond ring and gave it to him."

"You paid attention for once."

"But what do you want from me?"

"All of your research."

"So, what, you can claim it as your own?"

"Finally, the great Susa York catches up with her big mind."

Susa's head spun as she digested his words. "No."

Bernard scowled. "No? Then I'll have your cousin killed, and your precious nephew and sister. 2246 Willow Lane in Irvine, right?"

Susa looked at Bernard, horrified, then tried a different approach. "I don't understand, Bernard. You're a good scientist in your own right. How about we take a look at your research. I bet if we put our heads together, we could make your work stand out."

"You just said the operative word. Good. You're excellent. Once I finish presenting your research in my journal article, I'll be famous."

"You've been writing about my findings? But I'm not even sure about them. I have more studies to conduct."

"That's why you're going to tell me all about those studies. I can take over where you left off."

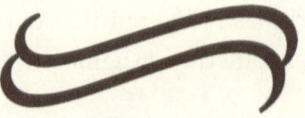

Kent heard a vehicle coming from a distance. Quickly, he pulled the box out of the earth and put back the soil, patting it down as best he could. Then he ran to a cover of trees.

An SUV appeared and stopped next to the tree. A muscular guy got out of the driver's side and pulled open a back door. Then a tall guy with blond hair and an ill-fitting jacket emerged. It looked like Hermann.

The man handed Hermann a shovel, then pushed him toward the tree, where he began digging. After a few minutes, Hermann got to his hands and knees and started frantically pawing the earth. After a minute of searching the ground, he cried, "Someone must have gotten to them."

The man kicked Hermann hard in the side, sending him sprawling sideways and howling. Then he took out his phone and dialed a number, growling into the phone for a moment. When he hung up, he announced, "The boss said you've outworn your welcome." Taking out his gun, he aimed it at a cowering Hermann.

29

Just as the man cocked the gun, Kent charged at him from behind the tree where he'd been hiding. As the man swung around, Kent lowered the tire iron against his head and knocked him to the ground. The man shuddered, then lay still.

"Rogue!" cried Hermann. He got up from the ground. "Is he dead?"

Kent kneeled and checked the man's pulse. "No." He picked the goon's gun up, uncocked it, and slipped it into the back of his pants. Then he stood to face Hermann. "Where's Susa?"

"I don't know. A man took her from Aunt Marion's house."

"Who took her?"

"His name is Hewes. Then that goon brought me out here. I told them the diamonds were buried here."

Kent pulled the box, caked in mud and soggy, from his pocket and showed Hermann. "The stuff is still in there."

Hermann's eyes lit up. "There's a diamond in there worth a fortune. We might be able to get Susa back with it."

"Once we figure out where she is." Just then, Kent's phone buzzed. He pulled it out of his pocket. A text from Joey. *Got some interesting info off a surveillance camera.* Kent dialed Joey's number.

"Kent. You get to Georgia okay?"

"Yeah, and I've got Hermann, but no Susa."

"Listen, the surveillance outside of the lab shows Hermann stashing the diamonds behind the trash can, then a funny thing happens. This guy who works at the lab with Susa, Bernard Holmes, comes and checks the bag, then puts it back where it was. I looked him up. His father owns companies all over Georgia, and his uncle is none other than Hewes. I'll text you the addresses."

Kent slipped his phone into his pocket. "I think I know who has Susa. A guy by the name of Bernard Holmes."

Hermann gasped. "Bernard? His parents own the ring in your pocket. It's a long story, but he gave it to me that summer."

Bernard stood towering over Susa, who sat at a microscope with materials he had stolen from her workspace in Irvine, including her notebook.

"You're going to tell me what everything in here means." He set the notebook in front of her, flipping to the recent jimsonweed study. "Are you saying the jimsonweed assay could indicate a connection with addictions?"

Susa couldn't give this information to Bernard. It was ground-breaking.

"Your silence speaks volumes," said Bernard, his voice taking on an animated tone. He made some notations in her notebook. "Now tell me about these formulas." He turned to some of her earlier findings.

"What is your plan, Bernard? To go back to UCI and tell them you discovered what they already know I've been working on?"

Bernard sighed. "I'm not going back to that stupid lab. I'm going to claim this work as mine. A few people at the lab who know what you're doing have been paid off. Those who wouldn't take the payoff, like your director, are going to find themselves in unfortunate accidents."

Susa gasped. "This research is meant to help people, not hurt them."

"If you don't want your sister and nephew to be hurt, you better keep telling me everything I need to know. And if you think someone is coming to your rescue, forget it. Hermann is being held until my uncle and father get the diamonds. And that boyfriend of yours is looking around Southern California for you. By the time he figures out what has happened, this will all be over."

Susa thought of Kent and Hermann and her sister and Devan and a lump formed in her throat.

Kent poured over a map with the addresses Joey had sent him. Holmes's largest piece of land was nearby. Kent steered the car onto the road.

"What would Bernard want with Susa?" asked Hermann as they drove. "Do you think he regrets giving me that diamond twenty years ago and wants to see if I still have it?"

Suddenly, everything came together for Kent. "Susa said something to me about not trusting everyone she works with." He looked at Hermann.

"Oh, my god. He wants her work?"

"Hold on," said Kent, gunning the engine and praying that this time he was heading for Susa.

When Kent neared the property, he slowed down.

"Any plan?" said Hermann.

"None, but I'm good at improvising." Eventually the drive led them to a massive metal gate.

"Now what?" whispered Hermann.

"Wave," said Kent, noting multiple cameras atop the gate.

Hermann gave a tentative wave out the car window.

"We're in the South where it's, shoot trespassers first, ask questions later. We're better off introducing ourselves," said Kent.

Before long, a vehicle approached on the other side of the gate, and it swung open. Two armed men got out of an SUV and headed toward them.

Kent put the gun under the front seat. "Great, now we've lost our only weapon," he muttered as the men came to the sides of the car and opened the doors, motioning for them to get out.

"What do you want, and who are you?" said one guard.

"To see Mr. Holmes. He knows who we are," said Kent.

One guard walked away to make a call, while the other guard motioned for them to come around to the front of the sedan and held them at gunpoint. When the first guard returned, he pointed with his gun for them to get in the back of the SUV. Then both guards got in the front, and the guard driving turned the vehicle around and headed for a low-slung industrial style building. Stopping short out front, the guard in the passenger seat barked for them to head into the building.

When they got inside, they were greeted by a middle-aged man with a paunch and shock of white hair.

"Mr. Aronson and St. James. What brings you here on this holiday night?"

"We want Susa," Kent demanded.

"What makes you think she's here?"

"We know she's in the lab with your son, Bernard. And we know what he wants. But Susa already gave her findings to a researcher at NIH. Your son is going to be found out as a fraud."

The man hesitated, then snorted. "That idiot. I told him that might be the case. We'll have to get rid of that researcher, too. This whole thing has gotten rather messy. You realize you've given me no choice but to get rid of all of you tonight? A most unpleasant thing on Christmas Eve."

"I wouldn't suggest that." Kent pulled the old box out of his jeans pocket, removing the heirloom diamond. He held the ring up to the light.

The man moved quickly toward them and snatched it from Kent. "This has been missing for decades."

"I also have your purple diamonds." Kent pulled out the bag with the single purple diamond and handed it to Holmes, who shook it out onto his hand.

"My, you're full of surprises." His tone became excited as he held the diamond up to the light. "Where are the rest?"

"Let Susa and Hermann go, and I'll give you the rest."

"What makes you think you can bargain with me?"

"I have nothing to lose. My sister and her husband have been put in protective custody. The only other person I care about is in this building. I get proof she's free and safe, I'll tell you where the diamonds are."

Holmes checked out the gems in his hand and appeared to consider Kent's words. He started to reply, when a bloodcurdling scream came from a nearby set of double doors. Holmes turned and rushed through the doors, Kent and Hermann following behind him. When they entered a large lab, Bernard was holding his hand, covered in sizzling flames. Kent spotted Susa running toward a back door and disappearing through it.

He and Hermann ran after her, while Holmes tried to help his son.

When they entered a back parking lot, Susa was already heading for the forested surroundings.

"Susa, Stop!" Kent shouted.

30

When Susa had given Bernard the assay to put in the kiln, she knew it was highly flammable, but was shocked when his hand lit on fire. There must have been some kind of residue from a project on his skin. She knew this might be her only chance for escape, so she sprinted toward the back of the laboratory. When she pushed her way through the emergency exit door, the winter air hit her in the face. As she ran toward the forest, she heard a familiar voice calling her name. She stopped and turned to see Kent and Hermann running toward her.

"Hermann, you're okay!" she said, feeling like both laughing and crying at the same time. Then she ran into Kent's strong embrace. "I can't believe you found me."

Kent pulled back and took her face in his hands. "Are you okay?" he asked.

Susa nodded.

"We need to get out of here," Hermann reminded them. "They've probably already called in reinforcements."

"There's a truck." Susa pointed across the parking lot. Snow flurries were starting to fall.

"I can hot-wire it," said Kent as they raced over to the vehicle. Just as he got a charge to the ignition, one of the guards appeared at the edge of the lot.

"Get in!" Kent shouted. Hermann and Susa piled into the back of the truck cab, and Kent peeled out of the parking lot and down the driveway. When a shot fired out and a loud metal ping hit the side of the truck, Kent yelled, "Get down, and hold on."

Susa clung to Hermann and braced herself as they neared the entry gate. The tires screeched when they hit the metal and the truck shuddered. She ducked down and heard a popping sound, then a loud crash as the truck lurched forward and more shots peppered the back window. Then the truck climbed up and over what must have been the gate and headed down the road.

Susa's heart pounded in her ears as she stayed crouched behind the seat, Hermann's breathing coming fast next to her.

"Is it safe to sit up?" Hermann asked after a few minutes.

"I think so," said Kent.

Susa peeked out the window to see the town approaching. Kent turned at a sign for the police station. When they got there, they found two FBI agents who had evidently been tailing them and had already stopped Hewes at the airfield before he could take off for a flight to Belize with his mistress. Other agents were in the process of apprehending Holmes and Bernard.

After they told them all they knew, one of the agents asked, "Will you folks be around for a few days in case we have more questions? Do you have somewhere to stay?"

"We can stay in my Aunt Marion's cabin in case you need us," said Susa. "It's not far from town. If we can get a ride there, we'll sort out the rental car in the morning."

As they waited in the station for their ride to the cabin, Kent called Joey to update him while Hermann got them all coffees.

"I know this is probably awful, but I figured something warm right about now would help." Hermann sat down to sip his coffee and grimaced.

"Well, for once, Hermann, we can safely say that you didn't get us into this mess, after all," said Susa. "It looks like they were using the stolen diamonds to get to my research."

Hermann contemplated for a moment. "You're right, although they wouldn't have had the in without my penchant for diamonds."

Kent hung up the phone. "Joey said the purple diamonds are going to be returned to the jeweler in LA once the one I gave to Holmes is returned. It looks like they did steal the purple diamonds to involve Hermann and then Susa, with the final plan being for Hewes and Holmes to sell the gems and Bernard to get your research. The jeweler wasn't talking, because they threatened to kill his family."

"What happens with the gem that was buried all those years?" asked Hermann.

"Oh, that was the other thing," said Kent. "It looks like that ring rightfully belongs to Bernard's mother's side of the family. His parents divorced several years ago."

"What a tangled web," said Hermann. "And it all started here at the lake."

When they got to Aunt Marion's house, the enormity of what had just happened finally hit Susa, who found herself feeling lightheaded on the front porch.

"You okay?" asked Kent. "Let's go inside."

Susa looked at the porch swing where she and Hermann had all their heart-to-hearts. "I think I'd like to stay here and catch my breath. Look out at the snow. I don't think I've ever seen a snowy Christmas Eve." She sat down on the swing, and Kent sat down next to her.

"It's Christmas now," said Hermann, who walked to the edge of the porch and stuck his tongue out to catch the flakes. "Look at the moon," he said, pointing, then he swung around and faced them. "Well, here we three are again. Just like I predicted."

"I have to admit that it all seemed like hocus-pocus when we did those ceremonies that summer, but there might be something to it," said Susa.

Hermann raised an eyebrow. "That from the scientist. You're my witness, Kent."

Kent laughed.

"There's a blanket in the front room," said Susa to her cousin. "Can you go in and get it?"

"Oh, I don't need to keep warm, hon. I'm still fired up from our adventure."

"For me and Kent," said Susa, giving Hermann a meaningful look.

"Oh, of course." Hermann winked at her and went in through the front door, then came back with a knitted afghan Aunt Marion had made many summers ago. "Let me put this around you two lovebirds, then I'm going to go in and call Brad. I'm banking on him thinking that it's pretty hot to have a boyfriend who's such a badass."

When the front door shut, Kent spoke. "I can't tell you how worried I was about you."

"I'm sorry. I shouldn't have gone off thinking I could save Hermann on my own. I was just so upset."

"That huge heart of yours is exactly why I fell in love with you." Kent stopped and held his breath, realizing he'd said more than he meant to. He waited for what seemed like an eternity, then Susa spoke, so quietly that Kent almost didn't hear her.

"I've always loved you. Since the day you first looked at me," she said. "I've loved you all these years. And now you're saying you love me, too?" Susa looked into Kent's eyes.

"Of course, I love you. I've always loved you," said Kent. "From the day you first looked at me." He pulled Susa tight against him, felt her body fit snugly next to his.

"I love you, I love you, I love you," she whispered against his ear, filling his heart to overflowing. Susa might just change his relationship with Christmas, he thought, pulling the blanket tightly around them both as the snow started falling in earnest.

EPILOGUE

Kent and Susa's stories are complete, but Ernesto's is just beginning...

Ernesto had no idea how he'd managed to get himself in a bar fight. He'd been working so hard to walk the straight and narrow. He'd only stepped into the bar for a drink, and now this.

But there was something not right about the guy who started the fight. The girl with him. She didn't look well. He'd seen this kind of thing before during his gang banging days, and he wondered if the guy was forcing her to be a drug mule. That's why he'd asked the questions and tried to get her alone to see if she was okay. But the jerk made it out as if Ernesto was after his girl. And now Ernesto was nursing what could be a broken nose, and the cholo and girl had disappeared.

"You want more ice, *mi amor*," asked the waitress, a curvy beauty with long, black, wavy hair just like Ernesto liked.

"Nah, I'll be okay."

"You stick around until after my shift, I can make sure you're going to be okay," she purred.

Ernesto considered the proposal, but he had an early morning at the restaurant baking bread. He was curious, though, about her plans for making sure he was okay, when a woman came out of the bathroom at the back of the bar screaming in Spanish, *"Mucha sangre."*

Springing off the bar stool, Ernesto ran to the bathroom, opening the door to see a pool of blood on the floor and spatters on the wall and bathroom stall. Careful not to step in the blood, he walked over to the stall door, pushing it open with his elbow. Empty. He heard police sirens in the distance and left the bathroom quickly, nearly running into the waitress. "There's a lot of blood, but no one in there," he said.

"That man and girl. You think that's her blood?" asked the waitress.

"Maybe," said Ernesto, his blood pumping faster the closer the sirens got. "I got to leave. Raincheck, *hermosa?*"

She gave him a knowing nod. "You can leave out the back, if you want."

Ernesto made his way out past the bathroom. He should stay and give the cops a description of the guy, but he couldn't take the chance they'd check his ID. There were plenty of people at the bar who could give a good description of the man and girl. No one with the guy's DNA on his face, true. But Ernesto just couldn't afford to get involved.

Read Ernesto's story in *Discovered Lies*...

A NOTE FOR YOU

Dear Reading Gem,

Thanks for spending time with me, Susa and Kent! While each of the books in the Discovered Truth Series can be read as a standalone, it's fun to experience the progression and get to know the characters. The series progresses as minor characters introduced in each book become main characters in subsequent books. It's exciting to see what they'll do next!

The Discovered Truth series features complex, gutsy women and equally complicated, charismatic men who find themselves immersed in dangerous and intriguing modern-day challenges, such as human trafficking, drug smuggling, national security threats, and identity theft. When the heroine and hero meet, worlds collide and sparks fly, kindling unforgettable romance and intrigue.

Thanks again and talk soon!

Julie

YOUR OPINION MATTERS

If you liked this book, please leave a review on Amazon, GoodReads, BookBub, or all three. If you don't wish to leave a review or don't have time, please leave a rating. Every star helps!

STAY ENLIGHTENED

Thanks for reading! Let's stay in touch. Here are some ways to do that.

Check out my website: https://www.juliebawdendavis.com/fiction/fiction-books/the-discovered-truth-series/

Email me at Julie@JulieBawdenDavis.com

Follow me on Facebook and Amazon

Join my VIP Reading Gems mailing list here. You'll get a free copy of *Discovered Beginnings*, the prequel to the series, and I have regular contests to win books in the series.

Escape to Unforgettable Romance and Intrigue...

BOOKS IN THE DISCOVERED TRUTH SERIES

Discovered Beginnings:
(FREE at https://www.juliebawdendavis.com/fiction)
Discovered Secrets
Discovered Memories
Discovered Indiscretions
Discovered Liaisons
Discovered Betrayal
Discovered Denial
Discovered Distractions
Discovered Deception
Discovered Lies
Discovered Vengeance
Discovered Redemption
Discovered Obsession
Discovered Transgressions
Discovered Suspicion
Discovered Escape
Discovered Promises
Discovered Cover-up
Discovered Intentions

Box Sets

The Discovered Truth Series Box Set Books 1-4
The Discovered Truth Series Box Set Books 5-8
The Discovered Truth Series Box Set Books 9-12
The Discovered Truth Series Box Set Books 13-16

www.ingramcontent.com/pod-product-compliance
Lightning Source LLC
Chambersburg PA
CBHW022021170626
46808CB00003B/1007